'Don't you like getting your hands dirty on real patients?'

Leah stood up and pushed her plate back. 'I've finished, Dr Kendall.'

'Have I offended you?'

'Yes.' The look she flashed at him was pure anger. 'But then, that doesn't seem to bother you very much. There are reasons for doing radiology other than making money, and you know it.'

He nodded, ignoring her anger. 'It's a speciality of the brain rather than the heart, though,' he said thoughtfully. 'Without knowing your background it's a speciality I wouldn't have guessed for you.'

'You mean if you hadn't known I was the sort of thoughtless little gold-digger who'd let her elderly relatives rot.'

'Something like that.' He was watching her carefully.

'But then, you don't know me very well, Dr Kendall.'

Marion Lennox has had a variety of careers—medical receptionist, computer programmer and teacher. Married, with two young children, she now lives in rural Victoria, Australia. Her wish for an occupation which would allow her to remain at home with her children, her dog and the budgie led her to attempt writing a novel.

Previous Titles

DOCTOR TRANSFORMED
CRUEL COUNTRY
DARE TO LOVE AGAIN

A BITTER JUDGEMENT

BY

MARION LENNOX

MILLS & BOON LIMITED
ETON HOUSE   18–24 PARADISE ROAD
RICHMOND   SURREY   TW9 1SR

First published in Great Britain 1991
by Mills & Boon Limited

© Marion Lennox 1991

Australian copyright 1991
Philippine copyright 1991
This edition 1991

ISBN 0 263 77317 5

Set in 10 on 12 pt Linotron Times
03-9107-52000
Typeset in Great Britain by Centracet, Cambridge
Made and printed in Great Britain

CHAPTER ONE

LEAH's weekend of make-believe was over. On Friday Dr Leah Craig had become a farmer. Now, two days later, she had accepted the inevitable. The obstacles in the way of continuing to own this place were impossible to surmount. It was time to return to the city and place this apology for a farm in the hands of the auctioneers.

Warwick was waiting with ill-concealed impatience. Two days of rough living, of smoking fires and no hot water had threatened his easygoing good humour. In this rugged bush setting he had been like a fish out of water. His expensive 'casual' clothes and soft Italian shoes had prevented him from stirring from the house.

The engine of his Mercedes was already running, as if it too was impatient for the comforts of the city. Warwick and his prestigious car were part of Leah's successful city life, she thought ruefully. They were totally out of place on this ramshackle farm.

Despite Warwick's impatience Leah hesitated, taking a last, long look at the country surrounding them. It was the first place, the first home she had ever owned, and to discard it as quickly as she was doing seemed almost sacrilege.

The farm had been hacked out of virgin bush and, with the onset of the old man's illness, the bush had started to reclaim its own. Even the home paddock was bracken-filled, with tiny eucalypts starting their upward surge. Leah could see the green-grey sweep of the river from the track exactly as she had the last time she had visited this place, fourteen years before. Another year's growth however and that view too would be lost.

Warwick was waiting. It was time to go. Leah stooped to pull off her disreputable gumboots, then raised her head at the sound of another vehicle over the purr of the Mercedes. She straightened and watched as a battered four-wheel-drive vehicle came down the track towards them.

The man who emerged from the vehicle was tall and lean, powerfully built and dressed for the land in moleskin trousers, khaki shirt and work boots. A local farmer, Leah guessed. He would be thirtyish, perhaps a bit more. His eyes were a clear, intense blue, crinkled at the corners as if from too much exposure to the sun. A wide generous mouth set in the tanned face gave a hint of humour.

'Good afternoon. I'm Hugh Kendall.' He came towards Leah with his hand outstretched. Leah took it and found her hand enveloped in a grip of iron.

'I'm Leah Craig,' she responded. He must be a neighbour come to check on them, she decided. She gestured towards Warwick who remained seated in the car. 'This is Warwick Ronaldson.'

The big man turned to greet Warwick, but Warwick simply raised a hand in brief acknowledgement and turned back to adjust the controls of his car. Really, he was being a king-size boor this weekend, Leah thought savagely. All he wanted to do was get back to the city. It wasn't as if she had forced him to come. He had been as curious as Leah.

She turned back to their visitor. 'We're just leaving,' she said apologetically.

'So I see.' He was eyeing her appraisingly. His voice, when he spoke, had a soft Scots burr. 'I was wondering, when I saw the car here, whether the farm had been sold. I own some of the neighbouring land and I've been keeping an eye on the place since the old man died.' He stopped, his eyes still watching her, waiting for an explanation.

Leah shook her head. 'It hasn't been sold. In fact I own it. If you live near here you would have been a neighbour to my great-uncle, Howard Reece.'

His face went still, the hint of humour fading. 'I didn't know Howard had any relatives.'

'Well, he had me.' Without knowing why, Leah's attitude had become defensive.

'He didn't see much of you.'

'No.' Leah said the word with finality. Her relationship between herself and her uncle was none of this stranger's business.

'I see.' The man turned and looked appraisingly at Warwick and the gleaming silver car. 'You've just come down to check out the place and see how much it's worth.'

'That's right,' Warwick agreed calmly. He glanced pointedly at his watch. 'Leah, we really have to go.'

'Did you know that your great-uncle was bedridden for the last six months before his death, and in the local hospital for the last three?' Hugh Kendall turned back to Leah as he spoke. His tone was clipped and accusing.

'No.' She stood and met his gaze squarely. She was of medium height but even on the step she didn't reach level height with this man.

His gaze swept over her, taking in the defiance of her stance. She flushed and her green eyes flashed anger.

'I don't suppose you would,' he agreed slowly. He hesitated and then seemed to come to a decision. 'Only the neighbours and medical staff had any contact with him in the end. Certainly not his family.'

'As I said, I didn't know.' Leah was flinching inwardly at the hard, accusing tone of the man before her. 'I didn't hear of his death until the solicitor contacted me on Friday.'

'When you couldn't wait to get down here and see what you'd scored,' he finished for her. Leah gasped but the man was not to be stopped. 'It's a wonder you hadn't kept some sort of an eye on the place, at least for the past few months.'

He gestured out to the bracken-filled paddocks. 'If you'd made some effort you would have reaped a better reward at the end,' he said scathingly. 'But then,' he paused and looked back at Leah, 'I suppose that was a risk you had to take. If you'd come you might have copped the grubby business of caring for an infirm relative. I guess it had to be much safer to wait for his death before descending to see how much the old man was worth.'

'That's not fair.' Leah gazed at the man in front of her in stupefaction. She felt as though she had been physically slapped.

'Isn't it?' He raised his brows in polite mockery. 'I dare say you're right.' He turned and gazed across the home paddock down to the river. 'In the right hands this farm could be a good proposition. You should be able to get a tidy sum for it. Almost worth the weekend's drive.'

Without turning back to her he strode over to his vehicle, got in and slammed the door savagely. Leah was left gazing after its retreating form.

For a moment she stood unmoving. The attack had come out of nowhere, unexpected and vicious.

Who was this Hugh Kendall to come barging in and accuse her of uncaring behaviour? A neighbour? A friend of her great-uncle? She shook her head in shocked disbelief. He obviously had no idea of the relationship between Leah and her great-uncle. At the thought of the old man the pain of the past welled up again and it was all she could do to hold back tears.

'Leah?'

With an effort she moved her gaze from the track and looked down. Warwick was watching her with sympathy.

'Come on, love. Don't let him get to you. He's just a country hick who doesn't know anything about it.'

Leah didn't answer. She returned her gaze to the empty track where a moment before Hugh Kendall's vehicle had been. She felt sick.

'Leah!' Warwick's tone was insistent. 'Come on. We have to go.'

The first few moments of the drive were done in silence. Leah was aware that she was shaking. How dared a stranger, a man whom she'd never met before, judge her so absolutely? She sat with her fists clenched, staring sightlessly ahead.

Warwick finally broke the silence. With a calculating glance across at his silent passenger he started.

'Leah, ignore it. He's not worth worrying about.'

She nodded slowly, emerging from the blankness of shock. 'It's made me think, though,' she said dully. 'Perhaps I should have checked——'

'For heaven's sake!' Warwick spoke in exasperation. 'You didn't owe anything to the old man and you know it.'

'And he didn't owe me anything. He didn't have to leave me the farm.'

'There's no one else he could leave it to,' Warwick said firmly. 'He didn't exactly spend his life making friends.'

Leah shook her head and said nothing. The sour taste in her mouth persisted.

'I'll tell you one thing he said that's right, though,' Warwick said reflectively. 'It is deteriorating. We're going to have to get rid of it fast or we'll be selling a bush block rather than a farm.'

'What do you mean?' Leah forced herself to concentrate on what Warwick was saying.

'Without animals on the place the bush is starting to take over,' he said seriously. 'Even I can see that. If we want a decent price the sooner we sell the better.'

'We?' She shook her head, still trying to rid herself of the persistent image of scornful blue eyes.

Warwick laughed and took a hand from the wheel to lay it proprietorially on her lap.

'We, my love. I've been thinking about this all weekend.'

'Oh, really?' Leah's tone was waspish. 'I didn't think you raised your thoughts any more than two inches from your briefcase.'

Warwick's urbane smile didn't slip. 'It's all very well for you to indulge in two days' frivolity, but we can't both relax. I've got solid court appearances all this week and I had to get the paperwork out of the way.'

Leah nodded resignedly. She knew Warwick was ambitious. She too had always driven herself hard and it was one of the things that had attracted her to Warwick.

They had met at university, with Leah studying medicine and Warwick law. They suited each other, conveniently pairing when a partner was needed but respecting each other's drive to work. It was a relationship which Leah was loath to change. Warwick, however, was starting to apply pressure. He was a successful corporate lawyer and successful corporate lawyers, Leah gathered, had wives. Suddenly their easygoing relationship was being pushed to something more serious.

'I'll do some ringing around on Monday,' Warwick was saying. 'Three hundred acres of river frontage. We should get a good price.'

Leah shook her head. 'Warwick, slow down. I only found out I inherited the farm last week.'

She hesitated. Until Hugh Kendall's sudden attack there had been real pleasure in learning that she had inherited the farm. For the first time in her life there was a hint that she belonged somewhere.

It had taken her by surprise, this feeling of wanting to have roots. For Leah, who had drifted for so long, the feeling was new and unexplored. Ownership of the farm had given her a glimpse, a taste of something she had not even known she wanted.

'I wouldn't mind waiting for a little,' she confessed to Warwick. 'Everything's happened so fast. I feel like I'm really rushing things.'

'Well, it's not as if we can put it to any use.' Warwick grimaced. 'Even if it was set up as a weekender it's much too far from the city. And frankly, darling, I can't see me as a hobby farmer.'

Leah nodded agreement. Warwick's smooth good looks and soft hands were suited to the office and perhaps the occasional foray to the ski-slopes. Until the stranger's unwelcome visit she had enjoyed the weekend. For Warwick it had been a trial.

'It's not as if you're sentimentally attached to the

place,' Warwick continued. 'You've only been here once before, haven't you?'

'Yes.' Leah bit her lip. 'Once. Just after my parents died. I was thirteen.'

'Well, there you are, then. You can hardly have fallen in love with the place on such short acquaintance.' He cast a measuring glance across at her. 'And, Leah, if might just be a heaven-sent opportunity.'

'For what?'

He hesitated, using the time to steer the Mercedes around some deep pot-holes in the gravel road.

'Leah, one of the partners in my firm is leaving next month to take up a position in America. It means I'll be moving up a rung in seniority with the firm, but as well as that he's suggested we might be interested in his house.'

Leah was silent, staring straight ahead.

'I've been there.' Warwick's voice had assumed the smoothly persuasive tone he applied to his more prickly clients. 'It's in a good neighbourhood, set right back from the road with everything we need. Five bedrooms, a tennis court, swimming pool, three bathrooms——'

'Three bathrooms!' Leah choked back a laugh. 'What on earth would we do with three bathrooms?'

'My job's always going to involve a lot of entertaining,' Warwick responded seriously. 'And besides, there's not always going to be just the two of us.'

Leah swivelled in the seat to face him. 'Warwick, are you proposing?' The shock she had received a few moments ago was receding as she forced herself to give Warwick her full attention.

He glanced from the road and smiled affectionately at her. 'Not now, my sweet. Let's get you home and cleaned up, then go out to dinner and talk about it.'

Leah understood. She glanced down at her dirty jeans and torn shirt. The mirror on the shade above her eyes showed that her usually shiny mass of dark curls was windswept and matted, and a streak of dirt ran down across her face, marring the perfect symmetry of her pale skin. Her deep green eyes stood out starkly in a face devoid of make-up. She had spent the last two days exploring every inch of the property and, she admitted fairly, didn't look at all the sort of woman Warwick would propose to. For Warwick the setting would have to be perfect.

Leah choked back a giggle. It wouldn't do to laugh. Besides—the bubble of amusement faded and she acknowledged what she had been avoiding for some time—her relationship with Warwick could no longer drift. She would have to make a decision.

Perhaps she didn't really need roots after all, she thought ironically. On Friday she had been Leah Craig, a woman alone and reliant on her own skills to survive. Two days later she owned a farm and now she could become Warwick's wife. Why did the prospect leave her feeling chilled?

She sank back on to the luxuriously upholstered seat and closed her eyes. Some decisions were just too hard.

'What the——?'

Leah's eyes flew open at Warwick's shocked exclamation. She glanced over at him, and then forward to find the source of his shock. A woman was waving frantically from the side of the road. As Warwick hit the brakes she stepped blindly out in front of the car.

The brakes on the Mercedes were superb, which was just as well. Warwick's foot was flat to the floor. The car ended up slewed sideways across the road, inches from the elderly woman blocking their path. Before either Leah or Warwick had time to react she was at the driver's door, hauling it open to grab Warwick's sleeve.

'Please. Please. . .' her breath was coming in ragged sobs '. . .it's my husband. Please. . .'

Leah was the first to recover. She had spent two years as a medical officer in Casualty and her training led to almost instinctive reaction in emergencies. Before Warwick had time to reply she was out of the car.

'Tell us what the problem is.'

The woman looked fleetingly across at her and then back at Warwick, still seated in the car. 'I. . . I. . .'

'I'm a doctor,' Leah said. Her voice was firm and authoritative. 'Where is your husband?'

The words registered. The woman released her grip on Warwick and turned.

'A doctor?'

'Yes.'

'Oh, thank God.' She took a step towards Leah but faltered and would have fallen if Leah hadn't reached her. Leah gripped the woman's shoulders and shook her.

'Tell me,' she insisted.

'He's dying,' the woman sobbed. She gestured up the hillside. At the edge of a newly ploughed clearing, where the land banked steeply upward, a tractor lay at a crazy angle. Leah stared upward as the woman continued. 'He's trapped. I've rung the ambulance but it's volunteer service and Dr Kendall's out at another call and no one's coming.' Her voice faded to a whisper. 'He can't breathe. He's going to die before they get here.'

She was talking to herself. Leah was already running,

neatly straddling the low fence and then stumbling across the freshly dug earth.

It took two minutes to reach the tractor and another few seconds to locate the farmer. The woman had not been exaggerating. The leg pinning the man under the machinery was the least of his problems. The lower part of his face had received a massive blow. As Leah knelt beside him she realised that the desperate fight for life was nearly over. His breathing was almost completely blocked. Each breath was a whistling, gasping fight and the dreadful blue hue to his skin told its own story. He was conscious, but only just. His eyes registered Leah's presence and a hand moved feebly to grip with fear.

'I'm a doctor.' Leah returned his grip strongly, meeting his terror-filled eyes. 'Try and relax while I see if I can help your breathing. Don't worry. We'll get you out of here.' The words she spoke were meaningless, but momentarily he seemed to relax before the effort of the next breath sent him sliding into unconsciousness.

Leah worked instinctively. She turned his face sideways—she would have liked to roll him on his side but the machinery pinning his leg made it impossible—and by the time Warwick and the farmer's wife approached her fingers were searching his mouth, methodically seeking to establish an airway.

It was impossible. As the footsteps behind her signalled Warwick's approach she spoke urgently.

'The penknife on your key-ring. Is it sharp?'

'I. . .' Warwick was thrown off balance. He looked down at the bunch of keys in his hand. 'I suppose it is.'

Leah held out a hand for it, then flicked the knife open. It was a wicked little blade, about an inch long.

'Warwick, I need a biro. No.' She shook her head at him as he obediently produced a gold fountain pen from his pocket. 'A biro. One with a plastic casing. There's one in my bag in the car. Run.'

Warwick hesitated for only a moment. As unused as he was to Leah throwing orders, her voice held the authority of knowledge.

Four minutes later it was done, the roughest, dirtiest tracheotomy Leah was ever likely to perform. Behind her, Warwick and the woman stood rigid with horror at her action, and indeed, Leah was appalled herself. To cut an incision in the farmer's throat and insert such an object as the casing of a biro which, four minutes before, had been lying in the accumulated debris at the bottom of her handbag went against every surgical principle she had ever been taught. There had, however, been no choice.

And it worked. Within seconds of the casing's entering the trachea the farmer's breathing re-routed through the plastic. The breathing settled to a steady rhythm and consciousness flickered back. The awful blueness started to fade. For a brief moment Leah closed her eyes in thankfulness and sank back on her heels.

Not for more than a moment though. Even though her thoughts had been centred on his breathing, at another level Leah had been aware of the farmer's leg. It was caught and pinned. She couldn't see where the damage was but she was aware that there was considerable bleeding underneath the tractor.

'I need a jack.' She turned to Warwick, at the same time keeping her hand steady on the life-giving plastic tube at the farmer's throat. He was no longer there. Only the woman remained, watching her husband with desperate eyes. Warwick had retreated to the bush at the edge of the clearing.

'Warwick!' Leah's voice held no sympathy as she called him back. If he wanted to be sick he could be sick later when she didn't need him. 'I need the jack from the back of the car,' she called. 'Now.'

He glanced across at her and then away. Leah grimaced. If he'd been a nurse she'd have sacked him on the spot.

'I'll go.' The woman spoke, her eyes not leaving her husband's face. She could see what Leah was trying to do and no amount of squeamishness was going to prevent her helping. 'If it's in the boot I'll need the keys.'

Leah stared down at the knife in her hand, still attached to the key-ring. She gave a rueful smile and wiped it on her jeans before handing it over. She was going to look like a butcher before this was over. She squatted in the dirt, supporting the rough tracheotomy tube until the woman returned with the jack. Warwick also found the courage to return, carefully keeping his face averted.

'You're going to have to jack it up yourselves,' Leah told them. She motioned towards the casing she was holding carefully in place. 'I can't leave this.'

'We can't jack it up,' Warwick protested. 'The ground's too soft to support a jack.'

'We need some wood.' Leah's mind was sharp and practical, turning over and discarding ideas with light-ning speed. 'A solid plank of some kind.' She raised her eyes questioningly to the woman.

'I. . . I don't know. There'll be one back at the house, I guess.'

Leah's eyes were moving across the paddock. They

came to rest at the gate near the car. A large wooden bar was nailed to the gate-post, reaching down to the ground to brace it with triangular strength. The whole structure looked old. One good kick. . .

It took precious moments to explain what she wanted to Warwick, and the woman was before him in reaching understanding. Leah watched impatiently as they tried to kick and haul the rail from its nailed position, and could have screamed in exasperation as Warwick tried to spare the gloss of his Italian leather shoes. Finally the plank was in position under the tractor and the jack inched the massive machinery upward. As Warwick operated the jack, Leah and the woman were finally able to pull the farmer clear.

'Warwick, I need your shirt.'

'My shirt?' Warwick was lost, confused and disoriented.

'Take your shirt off,' Leah said firmly. She motioned to the woman to assist him, then held out a hand to take the shirt. 'That's all I'll need you for,' she told Warwick, her voice softening. 'Go over to the car and find another from the suitcase.' He couldn't help his stomach's reaction and she was aware that he felt humiliated. Now she no longer needed him she could afford to be sympathetic. 'We'll be all right now.' Leah turned back to the woman and started giving instructions on applying a pressure pad to the huge gash on her husband's leg. Luckily the woman was made of sterner stuff than Warwick, or perhaps it was because she had more to lose.

They had another five minutes or so before the ambulance arrived, five minutes to catch their breath and accept that things were no longer desperate. The man and his wife were Wilf and Edith Harvey. Edith introduced herself and her husband solemnly and, despite the pain he was in, Wilf managed to acknowledge Leah's self-introduction with his eyes. Leah had the feeling that if her hands had not been totally occupied he would have proffered a handshake. A gently devoted couple, Leah decided. It wasn't fair that such a catastrophe should overtake them. Still, at least now Wilf had a fighting chance.

As Edith had prophesied, there was no doctor with the ambulance when it finally arrived. The two volunteer ambulance officers regarded Leah's handiwork with horror. As Leah walked beside the stretcher, carefully supporting the tube as the men eased the patient over the rough ground, Warwick returned from where he had been waiting by the car.

'Leah, we'll have to be going.' He glanced at his watch. 'I've made a booking for dinner at eight.'

They were at the ambulance.

'You must see I can't,' Leah said briefly. 'If this tube slips. . .' She didn't finish the sentence but every one of those present knew what she meant.

'Well, one of the ambulancemen can hold it,' Warwick snapped. He had been badly shocked and his patience was at an end. He wanted this nightmare to be over and to once again be in control of an orderly world. 'That's what they're trained for.'

'Not for this we're not, mate,' the driver said firmly. 'Look, miss, you say you're a doctor and we believe you. As far as we're concerned you've done something we haven't a clue about.' He motioned to the farmer's throat. 'You've done it. You're responsible, and if you don't mind we'd as soon you stayed being responsible until we can get him to Doc Kendall.'

And will some backwater country doctor be able to

cope with this? Leah thought bleakly. She doubted it. She could be stuck here for hours until Wilf Harvey could be transferred to the city. Would her makeshift tracheotomy hold out for that long? She blocked the thought. 'Of course I'm staying,' Leah said out loud.

'But tonight——'

'Nothing is more important than this.'

'Nothing?' Warwick's voice was grim.

'Nothing.' Leah's eyes met Warwick's angry ones. There was an unmistakable message there. Warwick was not enjoying the sensation of being partner to a doctor. Leah frowned. How often in the future would she be expected to be partner to a lawyer? 'You'll have to ring and cancel,' she continued. 'Will you follow and pick me up at the hospital?'

'Have I a choice?'

'Warwick!'

He bit his lip. 'OK, OK. I'm sorry.' He motioned to the ambulancemen who were waiting to close the doors. 'Go ahead. I'll follow.'

CHAPTER TWO

IT WAS a twenty-minute ride to the tiny bush nursing hospital. As they settled into the ride Leah turned her thoughts from the irate Warwick travelling behind and concentrated on the problems the farmer was going to face. Wilf was going to need facilities far greater than a tiny hospital such as Carslake could offer, but the most important thing was to set up a stable tracheotomy before the long journey to the city. She winced at the thought. It sounded simple, to extend the work she'd already done, but the swelling to the farmer's throat would be greater the longer it was left. It was going to require surgical skills she was unsure she possessed. The procedure required two doctors. If the Carslake doctor had no greater skill than she had, Wilf Harvey was in trouble.

'Dr Kendall was out when we left,' the ambulance officer replied in response to Leah's query. 'He was on his way to a house call on a patient out the other side of Carslake. We left Matron trying to contact him.'

'Kendall.' Leah wrinkled her nose as she heard the doctor's name. Wasn't that the name the man back at the farm had called himself? She grimaced. With her luck they'd turn out to be brothers.

Matron, it seemed, had been successful. They arrived simultaneously, the three vehicles pulling into the hospital parking area one after another—the ambulance, Warwick's Mercedes and the battered four-wheel-drive of the local doctor. Leah recognised it as soon as she saw it and, with a sinking heart, acknowledged what it meant. Dr Kendall and Hugh Kendall, farmer, were one and the same person.

The big tanned man was out of his vehicle almost before it stopped, striding swiftly over to assist in swinging back the ambulance doors.

'My God!'

It was an explosion of disbelief as he took in the tableau in the ambulance.

In the moment of stunned silence that followed Leah reappraised the man. Certainly he had the outward appearance of a strong and muscular farmer. Her eyes dropped to his hands and she accepted as fact that this man really was a doctor. They weren't farmer's hands. No farmer's hands could ever be so cared for. They had the calluses of hard work, but they were scrubbed into meticulous cleanliness.

For a long moment he stared in shocked disbelief at Wilf's throat. Finally his gaze moved to take in Edith, the ambulance officer and finally Leah.

'You!'

Leah didn't answer. In the circumstances there was nothing she could think of to say.

'Do you know what you're doing?' he demanded. He had summed up the situation and come to the only conclusion possible: that Leah was responsible.

'I'm a doctor,' she said defensively. He was making her feel like a schoolgirl with his hard, comprehensive gaze. 'There was no choice.'

He swung up into the ambulance, looked for himself and believed her. Leah and the others crammed into the back of the ambulance were ignored. He took Wilf's hand and held hard.

'You'll be all right now, Wilf. You're in good hands.'

He had bent over Wilf, confronting directly the pain-racked eyes of the figure on the stretcher. 'We're going to fill you full of pain-killers and they're going to make you pretty sleepy. While you're nice and dozy we'll do a bit of urgent repair work.' He smiled reassuringly down at the farmer. 'As good as this ingenious little breathing tube is, we'll put in one that you can claim on your health insurance. There's no category for biros.'

A tiny flicker of humour in Wilf's eyes showed that he was still aware. Dr Kendall didn't take his eyes from the farmer's face.

'After the pain-killer you'll be drifting in and out of sleep, Wilf. You'll probably be aware of our putting you into an aeroplane for a trip to the city hospital. By the look of it you've smashed your jaw pretty soundly and, if we're going to turn you back into the man Edith married, I think we'd better have it set by experts.' He motioned towards Edith. 'We'll organise it so that when you wake up Edith'll be there too.'

It was enough. Wilf's eyes closed. The big man leaned forward and put a gentle hand on Edith's shoulder. She had quietly started to weep, hunched miserably in the corner of the van. 'We'll have him right, Edith. Trust me.' Then he was gone, barking orders as he strode down the hospital corridor.

Leah stayed where she was, unmoving, until the theatre was ready. The swelling around Wilf's throat was increasing all the time and Leah was becoming increasingly nervous. Her personal reaction to Hugh Kendall was forgotten. Her only thought of him at the moment was the desperate hope that he had surgical skill.

She sat, her hand immobile at Wilf's throat. Somewhere out there Warwick would be waiting impatiently but she couldn't help that. He would just have to wait.

If the tube was going to block it would most likely do so as Wilf was being moved. To Leah's relief Hugh Kendall seemed aware of the risks and wanted everything ready before moving the stretcher. Finally the ambulancemen were given the signal and the stretcher was carefully pulled from the vehicle.

Warwick was waiting. As the team started to move through the door of Casualty he came forward and put a restraining hand on Leah's shoulder.

'Get out of the way!' Dr Kendall snapped. The doctor was treating Leah as if she were welded to her biro. 'Get on,' he signalled to the ambulancemen. 'Keep moving.'

'Leah, we have to go.'

Leah shook her head mutely, her eyes not leaving the position she had been watching for the last half-hour. Reaction was starting to take its toll and she was incapable of arguing.

'Get out of here or I'll pick you up and throw you out,' Dr Kendall said grimly. 'Go and polish your pretty car until I separate your girlfriend from her pen.'

Warwick stared at him for a long moment, his anger almost palpable. Leah flushed crimson. This man's social skills left a lot to be desired. He had just made an enemy. The stretcher moved on, leaving Warwick staring after them rigid with fury.

Because Leah's hold on the fragile breathing tube was so important she couldn't scrub for Theatre. She and her dubious piece of tubing were regarded as one item, not to be jolted or interfered with until a more satisfactory solution could be found. Dr Kendall simply worked around her.

He hadn't been in this country very long, Leah thought. His voice had the soft burr of Scotland, a far cry from the harsh vowels of most Australians. What on earth was he doing in this God-forsaken place? And where had he learnt the skills he so obviously possessed?

His management of the situation was superb. While still sending orders streaming to the nursing staff behind him, he was maintaining a steady flow of comforting small talk to the dreadfully hurt man in his care. There was no question of a general anaesthetic— the breathing was too fragile. All he could do was apply intravenous morphine—then local anaesthetic while he swiftly cleaned and extended Leah's incision.

To insert a tracheotomy tube into an already swollen and bleeding wound was a nightmare piece of surgery that Leah would have been horrified at undertaking. She watched with her heart in her mouth.

It looked easy. Leah's fear of controlling bleeding into the windpipe was not a difficulty for this skilled man. He was too swift. After setting up the intravenous line it was only minutes before a regular tracheotomy tube was in place and Leah was able to step away from the table.

She couldn't yet leave. As she hesitated Hugh spoke abruptly. 'Scrub and help me with this leg.' It was a nasty compound fracture and was still bleeding sluggishly.

Leah cast a fleeting thought to Warwick and then abandoned him. Having come this far, she might as well see this thing through to the end. She scrubbed as swiftly as she could, donned theatre garb and returned to the table.

They worked well together, the harsh words of the early afternoon placed firmly into the backs of both their minds as they became absorbed in the task at hand. As they worked, Wilf dozed fitfully, his breathing now a solid, steady rhythm. For the first time, Leah believed he would survive.

At last they had done all they could to stabilise their patient for the long trip to Melbourne. Once there he would have to undergo extensive surgery to set his jaw and leg, but from now on the shock could wear off and his condition should improve. Leah turned from the table with a warm feeling of satisfaction flowing through her.

They returned to the sinks together, wordlessly peeling off their gloves and starting to wash. The big man beside her finished drying his hands and waited until she had done the same. Then he reached forward and took her hand in his. The judgemental gaze of the afternoon had gone; a look of puzzlement had taken its place.

'I want to congratulate you on a fine piece of medicine. Wilf Harvey's a lucky man.'

Leah flushed. The eyes watching her now were warm with approval and admiration. They held hers and she caught her breath. The flush of colour on her cheeks faded and still she stayed, locked in that gaze.

What was she doing? This afternoon this man had hurt her so badly he had made her want to weep. And now? Leah wrenched her hand away and started self-consciously undoing her gown.

'You didn't do too badly yourself in there.'

'Thank you,' he said gravely, still watching her with

gentle humour. 'Now, shall we go and see if we can't placate the boyfriend? He should be in a rare old lather by now.'

Warwick. Leah glanced at her watch and bit her lip. She had been in Theatre for over an hour. Outside the light was beginning to fade.

'Am I right in assuming you're from Melbourne?' Hugh was asking. He held the door for her to precede him out into the corridor.

'Yes.' Warwick was going to be beside himself.

'Is it imperative that you travel home with your friend?'

Leah glanced up at the man beside her in surprise and then wished she hadn't. His eyes on her were giving her goose bumps. She gave herself a mental shake. She was being a fool.

'Someone's going to have to accompany Wilf Harvey on the plane,' he said seriously. 'I can't. When the Harvey call came through I'd just been called to an elderly chap with heart pain. The ambulance boys should have brought him in by now. I really can't leave the hospital.'

'Which hospital will Wilf be taken to?' Leah asked.

'City Central.'

She nodded. 'That's where I work and have my flat.' Warwick was going to be upset, but by now Leah was starting to be too weary to care. With a shock she was realising just how little she had ever asked of Warwick. If she could she had always fitted in with his plans. Now she had given him a miserable weekend and was going to throw his planned evening into chaos.

Leah had predicted that Warwick would be upset but even she wasn't prepared for his petty outburst. Waiting in the tiny reception area with Mrs Harvey, he had been gradually building up his blood-pressure to the point of explosion. His pride had been torn and he didn't like it one bit. As Hugh moved to greet and reassure the lady beside him he launched into the attack.

'Are you ready?'

'Warwick, I'm not coming.' Briefly she outlined what was happening and why she couldn't come. He listened, his expression growing darker as she spoke.

'Do you mean I've sat around in this place for hours for nothing?'

'I'm sorry, Warwick. I have no choice.'

He stared at her for a long minute. 'I'll get your suitcase,' he finally said shortly.

Hugh turned from his conversation with Edith. 'I'm sorry to deprive you of your lady for the night,' he said lightly. 'It is only for one night, though.'

'And what would you have done if Leah hadn't so conveniently presented herself this afternoon?' Warwick's words were almost a sneer and the smile dropped from Hugh's face.

'Wilf Harvey would have died,' Hugh Kendall said quietly.

'So we all suffer from your failing to maintain an efficient medical service,' Warwick spat back. He wheeled around and stalked out of the waiting-room. Leah took one glance up at Hugh's thunderous countenance and disappeared after Warwick. In his present mood if she didn't follow him he was likely to roar off into the sunset and leave her here without a change of clothes. Angry words or not, she wanted her suitcase.

Leah wasn't able to placate Warwick. He needed time, she thought, to come to terms with what had happened and with the fact that there were situations where she was going to be more useful than him. She was no longer sure he would be able to manage it and for the first time their relationship looked in real jeopardy. She watched the Mercedes disappear with misgivings. For a long time now Warwick had been a stable part of her world. Suddenly that stability was threatened.

She walked back into the hospital slowly. There was no rush. It would be another hour before the air ambulance would arrive to collect Wilf. She felt odd— as if everything were happening to someone else, not to cool, collected Leah Craig. She looked down at her clothes. Mud and blood still intermingled. The theatre gown she had worn had simply been placed over the top of the mess. Thank heaven she had a change of clothes in her suitcase. What she needed now was a shower.

A smiling nursing sister showed her to a spare room where she could shower and change. Thirty minutes later she felt almost human again, and ventured out into the hospital corridor.

'Dinner's on in the staff-room.' The same sister indicated a room at the end of the corridor.

'Where's Mrs Harvey?' Leah asked. 'Is someone looking after her?'

'One of the nurses has driven her home to collect some clothes,' the girl responded. 'We gave her coffee and sandwiches before she went. Not that she ate much,' she added thoughtfully.

Leah could understand that. She didn't feel all that hungry herself. The events of the afternoon had left her feeling shaken and a trifle queasy. It had been a long time since she had coped with trauma such as she had faced this afternoon.

Hugh Kendall was alone in the staff-room. He had obviously been waiting for Leah before beginning his meal. At the sound of Leah's arrival the cook, beaming, came out from the kitchen, placing a large slice of chicken pie before each of them. Her obvious delight in having two doctors to feed instead of one was infectious.

'Now you just call if you'd like more,' she told them severely. 'Dr Kendall, you just look after this young lady.' She looked at Leah doubtfully. 'Perhaps I should have given her a larger helping to start with. She's all skin and bone.'

'She looks all right to me.' Hugh smiled appreciatively, his eyes resting on Leah's slim form. 'There's plenty of time for her to grow a bosom to match yours, Mrs Ross.'

'Get away with you, you cheeky boy!' Hugh received a soft clout over the ear with a tea-towel, and Mrs Ross took her ample form off to the kitchen.

It should have been a relaxed meal, a meeting of two professionals pleased with the outcome of their work. Hugh had obviously decided to shelve his animosity in deference to a job well done.

It was easy for him, Leah thought bitterly. He hadn't been accused of heartless, grasping behaviour. She bit her lip. Still, after tonight she need never see the man again. He was welcome to whatever he liked to think of her. She concentrated on the excellent meal in front of her.

Still she was conscious of an undercurrent of tension. He was watching her, it seemed, trying to take her measure.

'Where did you train?' Leah asked the question

abruptly, almost rudely, trying to put the man on equal terms with her.

'Edinburgh.'

'Scotland?'

'Where else with a brogue like mine, lassie?' He lapsed into a broad Scottish accent. Despite herself Leah smiled.

'So what are you doing in the backblocks of the Australian Otways?'

He paused as if considering his words. 'I prefer it,' he said shortly, and Leah was left with the impression that there was more to tell. 'It's not so very different from home, after all.'

'You mean it's wet for nine days out of ten and foggy on the other?'

The gentle smile returned. As Leah's eyes met his she felt the tension rise again between them.

It was those eyes, she told herself crossly, turning away again to concentrate on Mrs Ross's chicken pie. No doctor she knew had eyes like his. They were the shrewd eyes of a bushman. She looked up almost furtively across the table and then down again quickly. He was still watching her, the gentle humour still there.

'And you, Dr Craig. Are you Australian, born and bred?'

'I've hardly been further than Melbourne,' she confessed. 'I was born there, trained there and work there.'

'At City Central?'

'Mmm.' Leah wasn't raising her eyes from her pie. Her body's chemistry was reacting in all sorts of alarming ways to this man over the other side of the table.

'You're not still doing your residency.' It was a

statement, not a question, and was in itself a compliment. Leah was acknowledged as an experienced doctor.

'No. I've done my two years. I'm training to be a radiologist.'

He frowned. For a long moment there was silence. Leah had the odd feeling that he had withdrawn, as if from something distasteful.

'You enjoy it?' The words were curt, forced out.

'Yes.' Leah met his eyes but her short affirmative came out sounding defensive.

'It's a lucrative speciality.' The words were bitter.

'I'm not doing it for the money.' This man was judging her. She flashed him a look of annoyance.

'So why are you doing it? Don't you like getting your hands dirty on real patients?'

Leah stood up and pushed her plate back. 'I've finished, Dr Kendall.'

'Have I offended you?'

'Yes.' The look she flashed at him was pure anger. 'But then, that doesn't seem to bother you very much. There are reasons for doing radiology other than making money, and you know it.'

He nodded, ignoring her anger. 'It's a speciality of the brain rather than the heart, though,' he said thoughtfully. 'Without knowing your background it's a speciality I wouldn't have guessed for you.'

'You mean if you hadn't known I was the sort of thoughtless little gold-digger who'd let her elderly relatives rot.'

'Something like that.' He was watching her carefully.

'But then, you don't know me very well, Dr Kendall.' It was as much as Leah could do to get the words out.

'Neither I do,' he agreed equitably. He also had finished his meal. As he rose Mrs Ross came bustling back.

'What about dessert?' she demanded. 'I've made lemon meringue pie and if you don't eat it it'll be wasted on those dratted nurses. Honestly!' she exclaimed in exasperation. 'I can leave a refrigerator full of left-overs and one night shift'll go through the lot. They reckon they knit when there's nothing to do,' she added darkly, 'but I'm on to them.'

Leah smiled. 'If the rest of your cooking is the same standard as your chicken pie I can understand the temptation.' She glanced at her watch and looked a question at Hugh. 'I'm afraid I haven't time for dessert. I have a plane to catch.'

Mrs Ross nodded. 'Yes, dear, I do understand, and it's a good thing you're doing.' She leaned forward and gripped Leah's hand suddenly. 'Edith and Wilf Harvey have been my friends for years.' Her eyes suddenly brimmed and she sniffed. 'You come back here and visit, any time you want to,' she ordered, reaching into a large apron pocket for a bright red handkerchief. She blew, hard. 'Why don't you offer her a job, Dr Kendall? You're always saying how short-handed you are.'

'I don't think Carslake is exactly Dr Craig's cup of tea.' Hugh cast a thoughtful glance at Leah. 'Dr Craig has ambition, and the one thing that Carslake can't help with is a career structure.' Once again, Leah caught a note of bitterness threaded through his words.

'So why were you at Carslake this weekend?' Mrs Ross persisted. 'And with a suitcase. Were you staying locally?'

'At a farm about five miles from here,' Leah said

quietly. Then she added defiantly, 'My farm. I inherited it from my great-uncle. Howard Reece.'

Hugh turned away abruptly. 'I'll go and start moving Wilf. When you're ready come to the casualty entrance. You can ride in the ambulance to the runway.' He was gone, striding swiftly down the corridor. Leah stared after him before turning back to Mrs Ross.

'Dr Kendall doesn't approve of the relationship,' she said bitterly. The older lady nodded, her eyes appraising the girl before her.

'Howard Reece was a patient in this hospital for three months before his death,' Mrs Ross said quietly. 'In all that time not one relation came near him.' She turned and picked up the used plates before disappearing into the kitchen. Leah was left staring at a closed door.

She thought back to the last time she had seen Howard Reece. The pain was still a raw, aching wound. Her fingers clenched at her sides. Damn them and their instant judgements. Two tears slid down her white cheeks and she brushed them away angrily. She took a deep breath. Go and get your suitcase, she told herself, get on the plane and get out of here. Warwick can put the farm on the market and it's over. She need never see Carslake and its judgemental inhabitants again.

CHAPTER THREE

IT WAS late before Leah arrived at City Central and after midnight before she finally put the key into the lock of her hospital flat.

Wilf had been taken to Theatre as soon as they had arrived. For a while Leah had stayed with Edith, until fatigue had finally overtaken her.

Edith was exhausted, but she was not giving in. The hospital staff had offered her a bed but she had refused.

'You go to bed though,' she said to Leah. 'I can't sleep until he's finished in there.' She gestured to the closed doors leading to the theatre. 'Tomorrow I'll sleep.'

'I don't like to leave you.'

Edith laid a hand on Leah's arm. 'You'll have to work tomorrow, won't you?'

'Yes,' Leah admitted.

'Well, go to bed now,' the elderly woman insisted. She turned to face Leah directly. 'You've done enough for us, my dear. More than. . .' Her voice faltered. She looked away and groped for a handkerchief.

Leah found her own and put it into the aged hands. 'What I've done has given me satisfaction,' she said calmly. 'You're not to thank me. Tell Wilf I want a ride on his tractor when he's up and about again.' She smiled at the weary lady in front of her. 'I've always wanted to ride a proper farm tractor.'

'I don't know about riding with Wilf,' Edith said with renewed asperity. She had some spirit still left after her day's ordeal. 'He doesn't even know how to keep it vertical.'

'I'll tell him you said that,' Leah laughed. She bent suddenly and kissed the lined cheek. 'Goodnight, then. I'll come to visit you both in the morning.'

She returned to her little apartment with a feeling of relief. It was a spartan hospital flat but its familiarity was oddly comforting after the strains of the last two days. It hadn't just been the accident either, she acknowledged to herself. Her inheritance, Warwick's behaviour, his proposal, Hugh Kendall. . . Too many things for her tired mind to think about.

She didn't ring Warwick. She knew he would expect a call to let him know she was back safely. She crossed to the phone but her hand just wouldn't reach out and lift the receiver off the hook. Somehow she would have to soothe and placate him, build up his damaged ego. She couldn't find the energy to make the effort. Tomorrow, she told herself.

She made herself a cup of hot chocolate and sat back in an armchair to drink it. The flat felt strange, an unbelievable contrast to the grubby clutter of the farm.

She should put up a few pictures, Leah told herself. It wasn't right to keep the place so spartan.

It was because she never really felt at home. Always she was just passing through, living temporarily until her life moved on to the next stage.

And what was the next stage? She had been doing radiology for over twelve months. Was she going to stay here, become a career doctor? Or become Mrs Warwick Ronaldson? Or something else? Unbidden, the thought of Hugh Kendall flashed into her mind and stayed. His deep blue eyes enveloped her and she closed her eyes and drifted. What would it be like to be kissed by such a man?

She opened her eyes suddenly, starting with a force that spilled her chocolate. What was she doing?

She was tired. Her mind was past the stage of being rational. With an effort she rose from the armchair and made her way to bed.

The image was still there. Fatigue was overcoming her, holding her head heavy on the crisp linen of her pillow, but still he was there. The hurtful things he had said to her were fading. As she drifted into sleep only the warm glow of approval, the Hugh Kendall who had gripped her hands and commended her work, stayed with her, colouring her dreams.

Leah woke late. She showered and dressed with speed and grabbed breakfast with the dexterity of years of practice at eating on the run. As she grabbed her white coat and left the flat the phone started to ring.

She knew who it would be. Warwick. She glanced at her watch. If she went back and answered it she wouldn't have time to see Wilf Harvey before her eight a.m. start. Warwick would have to wait.

Wilf's surgery had been successful, as Leah had anticipated it would be. His face resembled a scaffolded building, with wires and frames supporting the set jaw. Although he was still heavily sedated, his breathing was regular and firm. Edith had been sent off for a sleep and Leah knew that the elderly woman could at last relax. Her husband would recover.

At one level Leah was contented with the job she had done the day before. She should be satisfied and smug, she told herself crossly. Overriding her pride, however, was the bad taste left by Hugh Kendall's scorn.

As she stood by the bedside and looked down at the injured farmer, Leah felt a stab of jealousy for the resident in charge of the ward. She didn't want to be locked up in the dark-room with X-rays for the rest of the day. She wanted to be down here, making the decisions that would make this man well again.

The resident came up while Leah was standing at Wilf's bedside.

'Do you know him?' he asked curiously. He knew Leah was in the radiology department and knew that her place was not in the wards.

'I was first doctor on the scene,' Leah responded briefly. 'I had to do a very rough tracheotomy. I guess you could say I've got a personal interest in seeing how he's going.'

The resident looked at her with interest. 'How about that,' he said enviously. 'You know, it's always been my ambition to be around when someone yelled, "Is there a doctor in the house?"'

Leah grinned. 'It's a bit frightening when it finally happens,' she admitted. 'I think I like my crises happening where I can use a scalpel instead of a penknife.'

The young resident whistled in amazement and bent to examine Wilf's throat. 'Congratulations. It looks like he's going to live to tell the tale.' He looked up at Leah admiringly. 'And you a radiologist too! You don't even get practice with a scalpel in the radiology department.' His tone was disparaging.

'We do have our tense moments,' Leah said defensively. 'I gather you don't intend to take on radiology.'

'Nope,' the young man said cheerfully. 'My dad's a country GP. I know it sounds unambitious, but when

I've finished my residency that's where I'm headed.'
He grinned. 'My friends think I'm nuts.'

Leah smiled at the cheerful young man and left him
to his ward of sick patients.

Her jealousy stayed with her. The hands-on medicine
of the day before had stirred a well of discontent within
her.

'Don't you like getting your hands dirty on real
patients?' Hugh had asked. The answer was that she
did. Until yesterday she hadn't realised how much she
was missing it.

Ten minutes later Leah was in the radiology department of City Central.

She worked steadily through the backlog of films to
be reported. The weekend's X-rays were waiting. The
majority of them were straightforward, which was just
as well. Leah was not functioning at her best.

A brain rather than a heart job, Hugh had labelled
radiology. He was right, Leah thought, picking up the
next X-ray to scan for signs of invasive tumour. Surely
that wasn't grounds for criticism, though?

Perhaps her grounds for undertaking radiology
weren't sound. Why had she decided on this particular
speciality?

She enjoyed it. Achieving the skills necessary to
interpret complex images was a source of real satisfaction. Niggling at her now though were the arguments
Leah had heard Warwick put forward to her over and
over again. 'It's a job you can easily do part-time when
we have a family. And it pays magnificently, Leah.
You could support me in the manner to which I wish
to become accustomed.'

Leah had treated his words as a joke. Suddenly she

was questioning just how much she had allowed Warwick's approval of this speciality to weigh with her.

Leah shrugged her shoulders irritably and bent to write her report. She was allowing a complete stranger's disapproval to make her discontented with her lot. She looked down at the film in her hand and the small doubt remained.

A howl from one of the cubicles brought Leah from her reverie. She frowned. It was a child's cry. She glanced at her watch. Mary, the technician, was supposed to be doing a mammograph—a breast X-ray—in the next room. Mary was young and not terribly experienced. By the sound of it she could use a hand. Glad to get away from her own introspection, Leah put down the film and went to investigate.

Mary was out of her depth. Leah took one look and summed up the situation skilfully. A young mother had come in for investigation of a breast lump. Badly frightened herself, she had communicated her fear to her two small children who were reacting by clinging to the woman's skirts and screaming when either their mother or the unfortunate Mary tried to remove them.

Leah had coped with this situation before. The sign on the door said 'patients only', but some mothers just couldn't find anyone to care for the children while they underwent these investigative procedures. It was too much to expect frightened children to stay calmly in the waiting-room while Mummy disappeared fearfully with the white-clad stranger.

'Hi.' Leah spoke loudly, forcing the attention of the frightened trio on to her. Before the children had time to turn back into their mother's skirts, Leah dropped to crouch in front of them. Her hand disappeared into her pocket and came out with two bright coins.

'You know what these are?' she asked conversationally.

'Coins.' The eldest child was a boy of about four. He regarded Leah with an equal amount of scorn and suspicion.

Leah nodded encouragingly. 'You're right. They're not just ordinary coins though. They're fizzy drink coins.' Leah put a coin in each of her hands and held them towards the children.

There was silence. Four eyes gazed at her distrustfully.

'Fizzy drink coins are for something special,' Leah continued, her voice dropping as if imparting a secret. 'At the end of our corridor we have a great big red machine. It's full of fizzy drinks. Red drinks, brown drinks, green drinks, yellow drinks—you name it, it's in our fizzy drink machine. All you have to do is put these coins in, choose a colour for your fizzy drink and push a button.'

The four eyes didn't waver. Leah stood up. 'I have to take a photo of Mummy,' she added. She motioned towards the X-ray machine. 'See this? Isn't it the biggest camera you ever saw in your life?'

'It's not a camera.' The scorn was still there.

'It is, you know.' Leah smiled. 'It's a camera for taking photos of people's insides.' She motioned to a couple of enlarged films on the wall. 'They're not very pretty photos, are they?' The children's heads swung to the wall and back to Leah.

'Tell you what,' Leah suggested, smiling up at the frightened girl who was their mother, 'it's going to take me a while to take these photos of your mum.' She offered a coin to each child. 'Why don't you let Mary show you how to put the coins in the fizzy drink machine? When you've finished your drinks, come back and I'll show you a picture of a broken leg.'

It was too big a temptation. They looked up at their mother, doing her best to dredge a reassuring smile from the depths of her fear, and then across to Mary. Mary grinned her relief, took a small hand in each of hers and they departed to locate this amazing red machine. Leah heaved a sigh of relief. Once they were away from the contaminating fear of their mother, she could rely on Mary to keep them entertained for half an hour.

Leah performed a brief examination and took the X-rays. As she saw the results she gave another sigh of relief. She always checked the films before the patient left in case a movement or malfunction required a repeat. These films were fine and what they showed was fine too: a perfect benign little cyst.

'You can get dressed now, Mrs Lawrence.' She smiled at the woman. 'Mary should be back soon with the children. You can wait in the reception area if you wish.'

She looked up at Leah with panic-filled eyes. 'Do you know? Can you see what the result is?'

Leah shook her head. 'The results will be sent to your general practitioner. Most family doctors will ring for results of a test like this, though. You should be able to have the results by this afternoon.'

The desperation in the girl's eyes deepened. 'He said he wouldn't have the results until Wednesday at the earliest. I. . . Can't you tell me?'

This was the sort of situation Leah loathed. She threw a silent invective at the unknown doctor. Because he was too damned lazy to make a phone call this woman was going to have to live through two more days of nightmare. She met the frightened eyes in front of her and suddenly the rules of the department faded. This young mother was frightened not just for herself but for the existence of the little family surrounding her. It wasn't fair.

'It isn't cancer,' she said gently.

The girl's tear-filled eyes widened. 'Not?'

'Not,' Leah said firmly. She smiled. 'If it is I'll eat my hat and, as the only hat I own is a rather indigestible bicycle helmet, I think you'd better take my word for it.'

'How do you know?'

Leah sighed. She was totally out of order here, but having gone this far there was no going back. She propelled the woman into the dark-room and held up a film to the light.

'Look.' She pointed to a dark circular shape. 'Your lump is an almost perfect circle. If it was cancer those edges would be diffuse, uneven. And look at the density of the thing. It's an even density all the way through.' She smiled at her. 'That doesn't mean a lot to you, but to me it says that the lump you've got is filled with fluid. A perfect, round, fluid-filled lump is not cancer. It's a cyst, sitting there, minding its own business and doing absolutely no harm except scaring the daylights out of you.'

'Harmless?' It was a tiny, tremulous voice.

'Totally harmless.' Leah put her arm around her. 'And you know what? A lump that size would very likely not be a problem even if it was cancer. Caught when it's small it's no reason to write the next fifty years of living off your list of options. All the same,' she grinned, 'it's nice that it's not.'

'Dr Craig?'

The voice came from the door behind them and Leah's heart sank. Dr Raine. Her boss. She turned and met the older woman's gaze calmly. She was in trouble.

'Yes, Dr Raine?'

'When you're finished here I'll see you in my office.'

'It is not your job to give patients results.'

'I know that.' Leah stood uncomfortably in front of Dr Raine's desk. 'It was just that she was so frightened.'

'Many of our patients are frightened.' Dr Raine's voice was smooth and controlled. 'It is your job to obtain the best films possible to obtain a diagnosis. You are required to attempt to allay fears sufficiently to obtain that film. After that, the role of comforter is once again that of the general practitioner. Not us.'

'But if he won't ring for the diagnosis? If a patient has to live in fear for two days when we can set her mind at rest immediately?' Leah knew the answer to her protest before it came but it didn't stop Dr Raine voicing it.

'If the diagnosis is a bad one it's the general practitioner who is in a position to help,' Dr Raine said firmly. 'He knows his patients. Hopefully he knows whether they have family support, and can move to help them. Doing it your way you'd be telling patients you'd never met before, and had no time to counsel, that their fears were confirmed.'

'But Mrs Lawrence's results were fine.'

Dr Raine leaned back in her chair and looked at Leah. 'Leah, what is this? You know the score as well as I do. If we only gave results when the news was good it wouldn't take a fortnight before everyone in this city knew what not getting a result from the radiology department meant. If it's good news we'll tell, otherwise we'll pretend we don't know? What sort of system is that?'

Leah bit her lip and looked at the floor.

'Leah, why did you take up radiology?' The older woman's tone had gentled.

'You know why.' Leah had gone through this conversation before when she had applied to train in this department.

'I know why you've told us you want to work here.' Dr Raine held up a hand and counted off fingers. 'You enjoy the challenge of acquiring the necessary skills to be a radiologist, and the speciality of radiology fits in with your intended lifestyle. Mrs Warwick Ronaldson needs a job that can fit into normal working hours.'

'I didn't say that,' Leah protested.

'You didn't have to. It stands out a mile.' Dr Raine stood up and came around to put a hand on Leah's shoulder. 'Leah, you are a people doctor. You will make an adequate radiologist if you persist in this field but you're never going to be happy here. The only time I see you enjoying your work is when you're actually with patients. Radiology is not exactly a profession where you build up solid doctor-patient relationships, and, Leah, building up relationships with patients is what you're good at.' She smiled. 'I've listened to patients telling you their life-story five minutes after you met them. That's a skill for a general practitioner, not a radiologist.'

'I can't be a general practitioner if I marry Warwick,' Leah said softly. 'He'd never be able to stand the interference with his life.'

Margaret Raine let go of Leah's shoulder and stood back, watching Leah closely. 'Just be sure, then, Leah,

that marrying Warwick and being a radiologist is what
you really want to do with your life.'

By the time Leah had finished work for the day she
was exhausted. She made her way back to her flat at
the back of the hospital, then slumped into the big
armchair and sat, too tired to move. She was vaguely
aware of being hungry but couldn't find the energy to
rise and make herself dinner. While the tiny apartment
darkened as night fell, she sat and stared at the wall in
front of her.

Even though Leah hadn't ever agreed to marry
Warwick, she had always assumed that, at some time
in the future, that was what she would do. Cast adrift
after her parents' death, she had really formed no
attachment until she had met Warwick. With him she
had felt safe. Warwick had become her guide in this
risky business of life. He made no demands on her but
was always there.

It was Warwick who had suggested radiology as a
suitable speciality, and Leah, drifting through life as
she had since her parents had died, had seen no reason
to argue. Warwick was right. It was one of the few
specialities where she could obtain part-time work and
combine medicine with marriage. Now. . . Now she
wasn't so sure.

Why though? She tried to answer herself honestly.
Because of today and her conversation with Dr Raine?
Because of the accident? She had felt an overwhelming
sense of satisfaction at being able to help Wilf Harvey.
There was something else though, and Leah tried to
block it as it floated through her tired mind. It persisted. The thought of Hugh Kendall's eyes, flashing
scorn, stayed with her to gnaw like a tiresome worm.

The telephone interrupted her reflection. Warwick.

'Leah?'

'Yes?' Leah's voice was about as warm as an arctic winter, she acknowledged to herself, but it was too late to change it now.

'You sound delighted to hear from me.'

'I'm sorry.' Leah fought to inject some warmth and contrition into her voice. 'I've had one hell of a day.'

'On top of yesterday, too.' Warwick sounded sympathetic, and Leah realised he was trying to make peace. 'Can you come out to dinner?'

'No.' Leah bit her lip. She needed to be by herself, to think through the events of the last couple of days. 'Warwick, I'm dead tired. I'm going to bed.'

There was a long silence on the other end of the phone. Leah tried to make her weary brain find something to say but there was nothing there. Finally, Warwick spoke.

'OK.' He sounded wary, as if he was trying to judge the situation. 'We'll leave it tonight. Leah?'

'Yes.' Why did her voice sound so flat?

'I rang the estate agents who handle the Carslake district today. You'll need to go in to their city office and sign an authority before they put the farm on the market.'

Leah closed her eyes. 'Warwick, can we just leave it for a while?'

'For heaven's sake, why?' There was both exasperation and anger in his voice.

'Because I want to,' Leah snapped.

'Suit yourself, sweetheart.' The phone went dead. Leah sat looking at the receiver, knowing that it was going to cost her a huge effort to retrieve their relationship. She doubted whether she really wanted to try.

* * *

Once started, Leah's first steps at self-questioning opened up a floodgate. It was as if she had put her own will on hold for the last fourteen years, she thought scathingly. All the following week, as she worked or lay in bed attempting to find sleep, the questions went through and through her mind.

Since her parents' death, Leah had drifted. While still a child she had lived in a succession of foster homes. She had always been academically bright, and as her surroundings and the people around her had changed her school-work had been the one constant. She had gained a scholarship and had drifted into medicine. It had seemed a safe, secure future to a child with no roots.

She had enjoyed it. She might have drifted into it, she told herself, but she was right for the job. Her years as a resident doing one demanding job after another had been the most fulfilling of her life. By then though there was Warwick, another safe, secure anchor. And when the time had come to choose a speciality it had been Warwick she had listened to, drifting again into the option without risk. It was only the events of the last week that had brought home how badly she had been missing general medicine.

All week the conflict went on. Jumbling round her head were images of people, the frightened mother having her X-ray, Wilf who was starting on the long road to recovery, and Warwick. Superimposed on all these images was the gentle smile of Hugh Kendall slowly changing to scorn.

Leah started to feel as if she was caught in a kind of war. The sensible Leah Craig was advising her to ring Warwick and make her peace, and keep on her path of

radiology, wife and mother. The unsettled version of
the same Leah was backing with dismay from a prospect which had only two weeks ago seemed the only
choice.

CHAPTER FOUR

ON FRIDAY afternoon Leah finished her work earlier than usual. She was on duty for the weekend but she was free for the night.

Warwick went to his club with the partners from his firm on Friday nights. Still they hadn't made their peace and it didn't look as though it would be happening this weekend. He could come to the flat for dinner tomorrow, she thought, but rejected the idea before it consolidated. Warwick loathed it if she was called out mid-meal.

The weekend stretched out before her as a barren forty-eight hours.

At least she could see Wilf and Edith before she left the wards, she thought, and diverted her steps towards Men's Surgical. She had been dropping in on them all week and was becoming increasingly fond of the devoted pair.

She had done some urgent shopping for Edith during her lunch break on Monday, and at each visit was enjoying the transformation of the soft blue and white mohair wool Edith had requested into long lengths of knitting. Wilf was as yet unable to speak—there was still massive swelling—but Edith chatted to him, smiled and knitted, and Wilf smiled acknowledgement with his eyes and slept.

Leah pushed open the door to the ward and looked to the bed, then stopped in confusion. Hugh Kendall was standing talking to the farmer and his wife.

For an instant Leah thought of retreating, but even as she thought of it retreat was no longer possible. Edith glanced up at the opening of the door and stood up, her face creasing in pleasure.

'Leah!' Formalities had long ago been abandoned by the two of them. 'Look who's here! Aren't we honoured?'

Leah came forward, dredging up a smile. 'Very honoured,' she agreed. 'What crisis has dragged Dr Kendall away from the imperatives of his Carslake practice?'

Her voice was more curt than she had intended, and Edith cast her a curious glance.

'I haven't been to town for months,' Hugh said gravely. 'There was a conference on heart disease I badly wanted to attend.' He grimaced. 'It was a two-day conference but coming for the last session just had to do. It meant I could get the literature and talk to the people I most wanted to see.'

He met Leah's gaze calmly before continuing. 'If I never come near the town I'm going to be out of date very quickly as a doctor. Besides. . .' he looked down at the bed and his eyes assumed their lazy warmth '. . . I wanted to see the result of our handiwork. I think we've done rather well, wouldn't you say, Dr Craig?'

His eyes met hers challengingly, and Leah was forced to smile.

'I guess we have, Dr Kendall.'

Edith snorted. 'My, aren't we formal?' She grinned at them both. 'Not that I'm disagreeing, mind.' She poked her husband's stomach through the bedclothes with the knitting needle. 'It looks as though I'll be ironing shirts and cleaning up after muddy boots for a while longer, thanks to you two.' She looked fondly down at Wilf and his eyes smiled their response. His hand moved to grip hers.

The sound of the dinner trolley approaching down the corridor made her look up. She removed her hand from her husband's grasp and rolled up her knitting decisively.

'So where are you eating?' she demanded of Hugh. 'The hospital gives me a meal here with Wilf, or I'd take you out on the town.'

'You still could.' Hugh laughed down at Wilf. 'Wilf's hardly in a position to object.'

Edith smiled. 'No, thank you, Dr Kendall,' she said primly. 'My place is with Wilf.' She looked up at him and demanded mischievously, 'If you want to go out on the town I suggest you take Leah. It seems to me she gets about as much fun as you do, which isn't,' she added with asperity, 'very much.'

'I'm sure Dr Craig's boyfriend is occupying her this evening,' Hugh said quietly.

'Is he?' Edith demanded, turning to Leah.

'N. . .no.' Leah was backed into a corner and couldn't produce the outright lie she wanted to utter.

'Well, off you go, then.' The dinner trolley had arrived, and Edith's attention was diverted to more important things. They were dismissed.

Outside the ward door Leah turned to Hugh. 'I. . . Would you like me to show you where the cafeteria is?' She was floundering.

He shook his head consideringly. 'Are you really free of the boyfriend this evening?'

'Warwick goes to his club on a Friday night,' Leah said stiffly.

Hugh nodded as if he should have known. 'And you

stay home and wash your hair ready for the big weekend.'

Leah smiled in spite of herself. 'So I can look beautiful for all the X-rays I'm going to see over the next forty-eight hours,' she agreed.

Hugh's eyes narrowed. 'You're on duty over the weekend and still he goes out on Friday night?' he demanded. 'What sort of relationship is that?'

'That's none of your business, Dr Kendall,' Leah said quietly. Their eyes met and there was a sudden stillness between them.

'Well,' Hugh said finally. 'I haven't been to town for two months. I refuse to eat cafeteria food.' He looked at his watch. 'It's early still. What about getting out of that,' he gestured to her white coat, 'and coming out to dinner with me? I'll ring Stacey's and book us a table.'

'Stacey's!' It was one of the most exclusive restaurants in the city. 'You'll never get in at this short notice.'

'We'll see,' he said enigmatically. 'Now, what about taking me back to your flat and giving me a drink? I'll phone while you change.'

It was strange dressing for the evening in her little bedroom with Hugh standing on the other side of the door. She could hear his voice on the phone, a soft murmur, and laughter.

She pulled open the wardrobe and surveyed it consideringly. Stacey's. Despite her desire to not wish to appear as if she had gone to any trouble, there was no help for it. The place demanded formality.

She had a neat little black skirt and matching jacket which would do. She pulled them out and as she did so the soft satin of the white dress hanging beside the skirt swung out, as if demanding Leah's consideration.

The image of Stacey's hung in her mind. She and Warwick had gone there once when he'd been trying to impress an overseas client. It had been the wrong setting for a business dinner, small and intimate, with soft music and gentle voices. The loud conversation of Warwick's client and Warwick's clipped legal reasoning had jarred.

Leah took a deep breath and hung the suit back in the wardrobe.

The white dress was pure extravagance, bought in a fit of madness one Saturday morning when she'd been feeling miserable. She had walked past it in a shop window, gone and had a cup of coffee, walked past it again and bought it.

The dress was of embossed satin, cut low across her breast in a heart-shaped V. Its three-quarter-length tight-fitting sleeves fell from off the shoulder. The dress moulded to her skin like a glove, hugging her body and accentuating her tiny waist. It was calf-length, her slender legs finding freedom of movement by the thigh-high slash at the side.

She had worn it once for Warwick. He had asked her how much it had cost and she had never worn it again.

But Stacey's. . .

She opened the door a crack and peered out. Hugh had finished on the telephone and was flicking through one of her medical journals.

'Did you get a booking?'

He raised his eyebrows in surprise. 'Of course.'

Leah choked. The man was just too damned confi- dent. She shut the door and pulled on her dress. As it fell smoothly over her slip the same feeling came back that she had felt when she had seen it hanging in the shop window. Anything was possible in this dress. Warwick had soured it for her, but it was still there.

She brushed her soft curls and clipped them back from her face with two combs interwound with white silk. A tiny amount of make-up, the sheerest of stockings, and satin shoes, and she was ready.

It took courage to open the door of her bedroom. She was suddenly struck by an urge to pull the thing off and don the black suit. She took her courage in both hands and turned the knob.

He turned at the opening of the door. His smile faded and for a long moment there was silence.

'You did say Stacey's,' Leah said finally, almost defensively. She could feel herself flushing from her toes to her forehead.

His slow smile started again, warming the room. 'I did say Stacey's,' he agreed gravely. 'And I think I just might be going to enjoy myself.'

For the night the antagonism which had gone before was forgotten, or shelved to be recalled at some later date. Hugh seemed a gentler version of himself, determined to be pleased.

'It might be months before I'm back here,' he explained to Leah. 'Though tonight I feel akin to a starving man being fed Christmas dinner. I usually eat alone.'

'Here?' Leah motioned to their surroundings. They had been wafted to an alcove seat, one of the best positions in the house. Here they were cut off from the sights and sounds of the restaurant. Through the floor-length window shone the lights of the harbour, softly shrouded in sea mist. There was only the sea and each other.

He smiled. 'The proprietor is a friend. He's a Scot as well.'

Leah raised her eyes in surprise. 'I didn't know the Scots could cook like this.'

'It depends entirely on the Scot,' Hugh said wryly. 'Yours truly can cook a mean baked bean if he puts his mind to it.'

Leah laughed. She was slowly relaxing, lulled by the wine, the food and the soft burr in the voice of the man seated opposite.

The meal was superb. There were tiny brioches, stuffed with baby mushrooms and a sour-cream sauce. Mussels followed, in their white wine broth, and then lobster, whose tenderness testified to its having been caught that morning.

As sweets arrived—tiny peeled grapes in a crust of brown sugar and liqueur—Hugh's friend appeared from the kitchen. He eyed Leah approvingly.

'Well, well.' He beamed down at her. 'So the great Hugh Kendall's monastic pledge is finally broken.' His accent was more pronounced than Hugh's.

Hugh grimaced. 'Give us a break, Robert.' He performed the introductions with ease. 'Dr Craig is a medical colleague, with a nice safe boyfriend waiting at home.'

'More fool him,' Robert said bluntly. His eyes were frankly admiring. 'If I had Dr Leah Craig as a girlfriend I wouldn't be letting her out with Hugh Kendall, or anyone else for that matter.'

Leah blushed and smiled at this softly spoken man. On their invitation he pulled up a chair, and Leah was able to relax and enjoy the men's light-hearted banter.

Too soon it was over. Hugh looked at his watch and rose with reluctance.

'Unfortunately I have to return to Carslake tonight,' he said briefly. 'It's dangerous to leave for more than a day. It's hard to leave any time, but if I don't have a day off every couple of months I'll go mad.'

'More mad,' Robert corrected him. 'There are many who'd say that you'd have to be mad to go to Carslake in the first place.' He looked down at Leah. 'What about you, Dr Craig? Do you yearn for a country practice with the population dependent on you and you alone?'

'Our Dr Craig is a city doctor,' Hugh said wryly. 'A radiologist. Not for her the responsibilities and commitment of general practice.'

Robert raised his eyebrows. 'You're not being a trifle judgemental, are you, Hugh, lad?'

Hugh laughed shortly. 'I don't have to be,' he said.

Leah sat quietly in the passenger-seat of Hugh's battered vehicle. Her lovely dress was out of place in this disreputable machine. Hugh's words were echoing around and around in her head.

There was silence until he pulled up outside the hospital. For a moment they stayed, staring straight ahead. Then Hugh swore.

'Look, I'm sorry,' he finally said. 'As Robert said, I'm judgemental. Maybe I've standards that are impossible.' He frowned down at the steering-wheel. 'Anyway, after tonight you never have to see me again. You can go back to being a successful radiologist and wife to your successful husband. I wish you joy.'

'Thank you,' Leah said quietly. She reached out for the handle to open the door. As she fumbled in the dark Hugh was around at her side, pulling the door open for her.

'Goodnight, Leah,' he said softly. 'Thank you for tonight.'

'Thank you,' she said quietly.

'And, Leah?'

'Yes?' She looked up at the face above her.

For a moment he hesitated, then took her face between his hands and lightly kissed her lips.

'You are very, very lovely.'

Leah spent her weekend in a limbo of indecision. Warwick didn't come near her. He was punishing her, she knew, and in the past his tactics had made her repent. Now she was simply grateful for his absence. It gave her a chance to think.

By Sunday night the confusion around her was clearing. She didn't know what she wanted from life. She only knew that she had made two wrong decisions: Warwick and radiology.

On impulse she made her way across to Men's Surgical. Inevitably Edith was there.

'He's got his tube out,' she announced joyfully.

Leah looked down. Without the tracheotomy tube Wilf looked almost like a member of the human race again. He wouldn't rejoin it completely until the scaffolding was removed, but it was a beginning.

'Congratulations,' she smiled.

'Thanks.' It was a croaking whisper.

'He's going to be stuck with listening for a while yet,' Edith went on complacently. 'I haven't had this appreciative an audience for years. It's nearly killing him not to be able to interrupt.'

'Make the most of it,' Leah warned. 'It won't last long.'

Edith was looking at her consideringly. 'Are you all right, child?' she asked suddenly. 'You look worn out.'

Leah looked down at the concerned face and the need to unburden herself was suddenly overwhelming.

For the next few minutes she ceased to be a professional. These two people, old enough to be her parents, were concerned, caring and ready to listen. Leah found herself voicing her doubts about the city, her job, even about Warwick. At the end she fell silent. She felt foolilsh, rather as if she had exposed herself for the first time and left herself very vulnerable.

'So now what?' Edith asked finally.

Leah shrugged. 'I don't know. All I've decided is that I have to leave here. I have to stand back and look at myself, and see what I really want to do, not what is safest for me to do.'

Edith nodded slowly. Beside her Wilf listened and nodded too, his eyes accepting and understanding. She had been lucky to have these two to talk to, Leah thought to herself.

'Where will you go?' Edith asked.

'I've only one place I can go,' Leah said slowly. She had told them of her inheritance. 'I have enough savings to go there and sit for a while, until I come to some sort of decision.'

'Well.' It was a drawn-out sound of satisfaction from Edith. 'Even if it's only for a few weeks, it will be grand to have you close.' She turned to look down to Wilf. 'Won't it, Father?'

They had to bend to hear the whispered response but it was already written in his eyes.

'It will that,' he said.

CHAPTER FIVE

FOUR weeks later Leah was back at Carslake.

She had burnt every bridge she could think of. Her job at City Central had been taken over by an owlish young man of serious intent, and her love-affair with Warwick had been ended with a short insincere note renouncing him for his own good—Leah still felt guilty when she thought of it.

She still had no idea what she wanted from the rest of her life. The only clear decision she had come to was that she didn't want to be a radiologist and she didn't want to marry Warwick. Out of the huge confused jumble in her mind these truths stood out like beacons.

As her resignation took effect her comfortable hospital flat was no longer available to her. She had exchanged her small sedan for a serviceable utility truck, packed up her belongings and headed for the farm. There she hoped she could have a quiet few weeks to get her tangled thoughts into some sort of order.

It was the first time in her life that Leah had lived anywhere that she owned. The idea of a quiet time lasted a whole half-hour, just until she had swept the first room and let the sunlight stream in. Interest and pride took over.

The tiny Carslake farmhouse had been subjected to its first spring-clean in thirty years. Leah had worked like a woman possessed. Once begun, the place was driving her to get it into order.

Her last big job had been the stove. She had put it off as too hard, but a week after her arrival she could put it off no longer. It was her only means of cooking and to put a match to it meant the big kitchen was immediately filled with thick, black smoke.

The afternoon had been hot. Leah spent a disgusting few minutes unblocking the chimney—surely there had to be an easier way than her clumsy method—and then scrubbed for what seemed hours. By the time she had the stove burning without smoking she was almost as black as the stove.

The hot water service she had ordered had not yet arrived. It was a cold shower or a swim. There really wasn't a choice. She grabbed a towel and a bar of soap and set off down the track.

Below the house, on Leah's side of the river, the bank widened to form a tiny sandy cove. There was no need to don a swim-suit. The farm was Leah's. The only people who knew she was here were Wilf and Edith and they were still tied to City Central. Wilf was recovering but it was a long, slow haul.

Leah slipped off her grubby clothes and dived neatly into the welcoming cool water. The bush crowded right to the edge of the river, with giant gum-trees towering to form a canopy of green over Leah's swimming place. Dappled sunlight flickered through the leaves. Leah cleaned herself thoroughly, then floated lazily on her back and let her mind drift.

She had swum every day since she'd arrived. Her time in the water was a time for reflection, for searching for peace within herself and answers to the question of what she intended to do with the rest of her life. She had savings to last her for a few months but she was under no illusion as to her capabilities as a farmer. At some time she was going to have to return to medicine.

Leah wasn't sure when she first realised that the silence of the afternoon was being disturbed. It wasn't a loud noise, just a rustling as if of wind through the trees. Only there was no wind. Floating on her back, she looked towards the wild brambles on the opposite bank and caught her breath in dismay. A lamb had slipped from the sharp rim of the upper bank. Just before it had been about to hit the water it had been caught and held by the blackberry brambles growing in profusion over the near vertical river-bank.

It wasn't her lamb. The stock on Leah's land had long since disappeared. The land on the other side of the river belonged to someone else.

The lamb might not belong to her but there was no way Leah could leave it there. She eyed it with dismay. It was tiny, almost newborn by the look of it, and stuck fast. A bleating from the top of the bank caused her to look up. The lamb's mother was peering anxiously down, pawing the ground as if to test whether she could descend.

'Don't do it!' Leah yelled sharply and watched with satisfaction as the ewe backed away. One lamb in the blackberries she might just cope with. A great fat ewe was another proposition.

She couldn't do anything without clothes on. Leah might not have been country bred, but those thorns holding the lamb fast looked sharp. She rolled over and swam back to her side of the river. Swiftly she pulled on her jeans, blouse and plimsolls before diving back into the water.

Leah wasn't a strong swimmer and her clothes made

her feel unpleasantly weighted. She swam sluggishly and was relieved when she reached the other bank.

'Now, quit struggling,' she said nervously, staring up the bank at the trapped lamb. 'If I'm going to get you out of there you're going to have to co-operate.'

Climbing the bank was no easy feat. The only handhold was the brambles, and by the time Leah reached the quivering little creature her hands were already bloodied and raw. She blocked her mind to the pain. If she did the sensible thing and returned to the farm for leather gloves and secateurs, even supposing such things existed there, she knew that once she had gone the mother would venture down.

It took over five minutes to extricate the tiny animal from its thorny web. Each time Leah pulled away a bramble another would catch in the fine new wool. After the first couple of moments the lamb ceased struggling. Was it because it sensed she was helping, Leah wondered, or was the shock of its ordeal starting to take effect?

Leah was working with one hand, using the other to hold herself to the face of the river-bank. Her feet were precariously held by more of the brambles. It was a tenuous hold. A couple of times she slipped and had to seize the thorny wood to stop herself slipping down again into the river below. Each time it happened her hands screamed a protest as the vicious thorns cut into flesh. The pathetic woolly bundle caught above Leah's shoulders was still enough to make her ignore the pain.

Finally she did it. The last bramble came away and the lamb was free. Untied from its position, the little animal dropped. Leah released the hand she had been using to support herself, grabbed the lamb with two hands and fell. Instinctively as she fell she shoved herself back from the bank. Still gripping the lamb, she lurched backwards and into the water below.

As she hit the water Leah lost her hold on the tiny lamb. Frantic with fear from the drop and the feel of the water, the animal fought from her grasp. As Leah struggled to the surface it slipped from her arms and disappeared.

'Leah!'

It was a man's voice. Leah took a huge lungful of air and looked wildly about. The voice was coming from above. Her frantic gaze flicked up to catch a glimpse of a tall figure on the bank above her.

'It's a lamb.' She was half choking, half sobbing, eyes almost blinded by the water. She didn't have time to see who this sudden arrival was or how he had come to be there. All she knew was that she needed help. 'I've lost it.' There was no time to wait for a response. She took a lungful of air and dived to grope in the muddy water, searching for the lamb.

So did the man on the bank. His dive hardly disturbed the surface. Searching desperately below the water, Leah was suddenly aware of being joined by a diver far more adept than she. As she was forced to rise for air she felt him beneath her, moving methodically over the river-bed.

'Got him!' It was an exultant shout as the diver broke the surface. His muscled arm raised the bedraggled lamb high out of the water. Still shocked and struggling for air, Leah could only gape. It was Hugh Kendall.

'Is it OK?' she gasped, struggling to tread water.

Hugh floated on to his back. Placing the tiny creature on his broad chest, he inspected him. For a moment the lamb lay limp. Leah caught her breath in dismay and, as she did so, it stirred, then struggled feebly against Hugh's restraining hand.

'He'll make it,' Hugh said in satisfaction. He cast a quick glance across at Leah. 'Are you all right?'

'Yes.' The water was sucking at her jeans and she felt as if every breath was an effort but, without the lamb, she could make it back to her side of the river.

'Sure?' His brows were furrowed in concern.

'Sure.'

'Swim to the bank, then. I'll watch you.'

'But the lamb——'

'Never mind the lamb. Swim.'

She did, leaving him floating midstream with his strange little burden.

'OK?' he called as she pulled herself clumsily on to the sand.

'Yes.' It was all she could get out.

'There's a place where I can get up to my side a bit further upstream. The best medicine for this little one is his mother. A couple of hours in the sun and a drink from his mum and he'll be right as rain.' He waved a hand in farewell. 'Don't go away. I'll be back.' With one hand still holding the lamb firmly on his chest he used his feet to kick himself swiftly around the bend in the river.

Leah lay back on the sand and waited. She was incapable of doing anything else. For the first time she acknowledged to herself that she had been badly frightened. For a weak swimmer it had been a foolish thing to attempt.

What on earth was Hugh Kendall doing here? she wondered. 'My side' he had called the other bank. Did that mean his land ran right next to hers? She couldn't think. She burrowed back on to the warm sand, trying to stop her body from shaking.

Hugh was back before Leah had time to bring her trembling limbs under control. He swam as if the moleskin trousers and shirt he was wearing didn't exist, with strong strokes pulling him through the water smoothly and surely.

He hauled himself up on the bank near where Leah lay. For a moment he didn't say anything, just turned to peruse the opposite bank where the mass of torn brambles told their own story.

Finally he turned and looked down at the limp figure at his feet.

'What the hell did you think you were doing?' His voice was hard and demanding.

Leah opened her mouth to answer but no sound came.

'How much do you think that bloody lamb is worth?' he continued. 'Your life?'

'I couldn't leave it there,' Leah whispered defensively. She was very close to tears.

'No one was asking for you to leave it. All you had to do was get on the telephone and ring me. I would have found it anyway, if it came to that. The ewes are in mid-lambing and I'm checking them every night and morning.' He glared down at her. 'I could have winched them up without all this drama—yes, even the ewe if she'd gone down. I've done it before.'

'Well, how was I to know that?' Leah threw back through her teeth, struggling to her feet as she spoke. 'How could I be sure they both wouldn't have made it down to the river and drowned before you got your act together and managed your rescue? If they're your sheep you obviously look after them so well!' Her voice was laced with sarcasm.

'And how was I to know that it was you who owned the next-door farm anyway?' she continued. To her horror she choked on a sob and ground to a halt, tears streaming down her cheeks. 'Go away,' she whispered fiercely. 'Get back on to your own land.' Her hands went up to check the streaming tears. 'You'd be well served if your whole damn flock drowned.'

'What have you done to your hands?' Hugh's voice had changed. Ignoring her outburst, he reached out and gripped her wrists, pulling them towards him.

'I. . . It doesn't matter.' Leah tried to pull back. She looked down with detached interest at the bleeding mess of her hands. They weren't just surface scratches, she noted with dismay. Some of the cuts were jagged and deep. She wrenched back again but could not break the steely grip. 'I'll be all right. Let me go.'

Hugh was still looking grimly down. 'They're not all right, and you know it.' He looked around. Below them, on the sand, were the remnants of the pile of clothes Leah had discarded at the start of her swim. She had put on her outer garments to cope with the blackberries but her wispy bra and panties were still lying on her towel. Hugh scooped them up. 'Come on, Leah Craig.' He was talking to her as if to a difficult patient. 'Let's take you home.'

The walk home was a blur. Leah's hands were starting to react with pain, sending stabbing shards through her arms. Her exhaustion from her unaccustomed efforts had left her limp and lifeless. On top of the sheer physical discomfort was the presence of the man beside her. She had finally pulled away from his grasp but he walked strongly beside her, reaching out to assist her over rough ground. A couple of times she stumbled and would have fallen. Always an arm was there, holding, steadying.

She felt foolish and very young. All she wanted was for this man to go away and leave her to her misery. And yet. . . She cast an uncertain glance up at him. He was so damned big. Part of her was achingly sensitive to him, reacting with a tingling warmth to his body beside her. It was just because he was big, she decided, trying to suppress the feeling of almost breathless awareness his presence engendered.

Hugh was in charge and was in no mood to brook an argument. Leah was marched into the farmhouse kitchen as if Hugh and not Leah owned the place.

'A hot shower, pronto,' he ordered.

'There's no hot water.' Leah's teeth were audibly chattering now as reaction set in.

Hugh abandoned her and went to investigate. Two minutes later he had huge pots full of water on top of the newly cleaned stove.

'A bath it is, then,' he directed. 'The river is muddy and those cuts are full of sand. You're asking for trouble if we leave them uncleaned and there are too many of them to clean separately.'

As he talked he swung her round and started peeling off her wet clothes. The sodden shirt was clinging limply to Leah's skin, disappearing into transparency wherever it touched.

'I can do it.' Leah reached up to push Hugh's hands away.

'Not with those hands you can't,' he said firmly. 'You'll just start them bleeding again. Now stand still and don't wriggle.'

There was nothing she could do. He propelled her gently on to the old settee near the fire and pulled off her disreputable plimsolls. The pain in her hands was severe, but not sufficient to block out awareness of Hugh's hands on her.

He's a doctor, she told herself. I'm just another patient. Then even this attempt at reassuring herself was denied. As he fought to unfasten the stubborn metal catch at the top of her jeans he looked up at her. Their eyes met. Suddenly the uncertainty in Leah's eyes was mirrored in the clear blue eyes of the man at her feet.

'My God, you're beautiful.' His voice was not quite steady. Abruptly he rose and strode into the bedroom. When he emerged he was carrying one of Leah's soft woollen blankets; as he pulled the limp jeans from her body he tucked it around her and disappeared out on to the veranda.

Leah was left with every inch of her crimson with embarrassment and mortification. She moved her useless hands in an attempt to tuck the blanket tighter around her. A deep cut between her finger and thumb stretched and sluggishly started to bleed. Leah swore softly. Without her hands she was helpless. Tears of frustration and pain mingled on her cheeks.

Damn Hugh Kendall and his rotten sheep. Why was she here anyway? In the same way a lost child wailed for its mother, Leah was filled with an overwhelming longing for the city, her nice, safe little dark-room at City Central, even Warwick. In the years Warwick had known her he had never seen her undressed. Suddenly Leah was missing him dreadfully.

Five minutes later Hugh returned. Ignoring Leah, he went straight to the stove and started carrying the now steaming vats of water into the bathroom. When he was satisfied he returned for Leah.

'I can bathe myself.'

'I know.' He gave the ghost of a smile. 'You're almost grown-up now.' He reached out and took one of her hands in his. 'Come on. You're sandy and muddy and you're not going to feel good until you're clean and these hands are dressed.' He lifted a finger and ran it through a strand of damp hair. 'You've got blackberry briar caught in your hair. Now how do you propose to clean it with your hands in this state? Or are you proposing to leave it until your hands heal?' He lifted one of her hands again and grimaced. 'I warn you, they're going to be sore for a few days.'

She looked up at him, her face a picture of dismay and confusion.

'Come on, Dr Craig,' he said sternly. Only a hint of laughter in the fine lines surrounding his eyes belied the seriousness of his tone. 'Your bath awaits you.' Without waiting for her reply he leaned over and picked her up, blanket and all. Somehow between the kitchen and the bathroom the blanket was discarded. Hugh kicked open the bathroom door with his foot and gently lowered Leah into the steaming bath.

It hurt. The pain of the scratches which had been inflicted on her bare arms and, in some cases, elsewhere on her body through her not very protective clothing screamed in protest at again meeting water. Before she could bite it back a tiny whimper of pain escaped her lips. She closed her eyes and bit her lip.

'That's the worst of it,' Hugh said sympathetically. 'I made it nice and deep so all the scratches would hit the water together. Now let's see if we can soak the dirt out.'

Hugh had no intention of leaving Leah to soak by herself. While her hands and arms lay soaking gently in the soapy water he started working on her hair. Gently he eased the worst of the brambles from her tangled curls. With the debris removed he lathered her hair into a foaming mass, running his fingers through and through the long strands. Satisfied at last, he brought more water from the kitchen and rinsed it through.

Leah lay in passive submission. One level of her brain was screaming that she was crazy to be here. The other level had gone into a stupor. To oppose Hugh Kendall was too difficult. Besides, as the warmth of the water soothed her hurts, her body was responding to his ministrations with languid pleasure. It was odd, she thought lazily. Warwick's tentative lovemaking had left her unmoved. She had almost started thinking that she was frigid. Now all this man had to do was run his fingers through her hair and a fire lit deep within her, crying a need of its own.

The strong fingers moving through her hair stopped abruptly, almost as if their owner had guessed her thoughts.

'Let's see those hands.' Hugh's voice sounded unnaturally harsh in the tiny room.

Leah held out her hands wordlessly. With the blood and sand removed, the cuts and scratches stood out starkly against the white skin.

'At least they're clean.' Still the harsh, abrasive tone. 'OK, let's get you out.' He placed his hands on her sides and helped her stand. She stepped over the rim of the bath, hard against him.

There was silence in the tiny room. Tension was running back and forth between them like an electric current. Hugh didn't move. His hands still held her sides.

Wonderingly Leah looked up. Her wounded hands were held out from her body, forcing her breasts to stand out. Hugh's gaze dropped from her face, turned mutely up towards him, down to the tautness of her nipples brushing damply against his shirt and back again to the lovely mouth. As he groaned his hands tightened and his face dropped to join his lips to hers.

Her hands were forgotten. Somewhere the controlled, possessed Leah Craig had been overtaken, steamrollered by this strange, wilful body with only one desire: to be as close to this hard male presence as she could be.

Hugh's clothes were still damp from the river, and the moisture from Leah's body added to his soaking state. The cloth of his shirt might not have existed. Beneath her breasts Leah could feel the rhythm of his heart, beating fiercely.

His tongue pressed urgently, searching for passage inside the soft moistness of her mouth. Leah felt her lips opening, welcoming the seeking tongue.

Her body was on fire. Deep in her thighs her need was taking over, pressing her body closer, closer. His hands moved to hold the firm flesh of her buttocks hard in against him, making her feel the urgency of his own desire. She gave a soft moan of pleasure and stirred her body against him.

It was enough. The tiny sound was one of desire and need but it caught at Hugh. He stepped back as if from an electric shock. Leah, leaning heavily against him, would have fallen but for his hands which moved up to grip her shoulders. They stood, caught, held by each other's eyes. Again it was Hugh who broke the moment. With a seemingly huge physical effort he turned away to reach for one of Leah's thick white bath-towels.

Wordlessly he dried her, while Leah stood mute and still. She was lost, caught in a vortex of emotion and sensation. The feel of the towel against her skin made her shudder. Helplessly she stood, waiting for it to end.

There was a bathrobe hanging behind the door. Hugh finished his steady drying and then helped Leah into it.

'Have you any medical supplies? Bandages? Antiseptic?' His voice was harsh and gravelly.

'There's a medical kit in the ute.' Like most doctors, Leah travelled equipped for minor trauma.

'Go and sit by the fire, then.' Hugh disappeared.

By the time Leah's hands were anointed and dressed she could have cried with relief. All she wanted was for this man to be gone. With her hands bandaged she could once again fend for herself, even if there would be some things she couldn't do for a few days.

'Thank you,' she told him stiffly as the last strip of dressing was secured.

'One more thing,' he said grimly.

'I'll be all right now,' she protested.

Once again Hugh lifted a strand of damply curling hair. 'Tell me where you keep a brush.'

It was torture—to sit still and have this man run the brush over and over against her head. He worked methodically, using a comb to tease out the mass of knots. Leah couldn't have done it herself, she acknowledged privately. Left to herself, in her present mood, she probably would have cut the lot off.

At last it was over. Hugh ran the brush through one

last time, then laid it beside Leah's chair. He rose and looked down at her.

'I'll drop in tomorrow and check that you can cope.'

'There's no need.' It was a savage whisper.

'Of course there's a need,' he said quietly. 'It was my lamb you got yourself into this mess over.'

'As you said, there was no need, though,' Leah said bitterly. 'My efforts were totally unnecessary. I'm surprised you haven't suggested it was my fault the lamb was stuck in the first place.'

'It was.'

Leah's head flew up. 'I beg your pardon?'

'The lamb mistook the brambles growing out from the cliff-face as solid ground,' Hugh said softly. 'Blackberries are one of the biggest pests around here. They spread like wildfire. The only way they can be kept under control is for every farmer to get rid of them on his land. Every year I spray mine, and every year they keep coming back, spread from this place. All your river land is overrun with them.'

'Well, that's hardly my fault.'

'No,' he agreed scornfully. 'It was the fault of an old man who was past running a farm and who didn't have a single relation who gave a damn for him.'

With that parting shot he was gone, the door slamming hard behind him.

CHAPTER SIX

THE following hours were long and painful. After a
fitful night's sleep Leah woke to a rain-filled day. The
long stretch of hot weather had finally broken. She lay
in the big old bed and watched the pattern of rain on
the grubby windows. Everywhere she looked in this
house there was still something that needed doing.

There wasn't going to be a lot done this week though.
She pulled her bandaged hands out from under the
covers and surveyed them ruefully. It had been as
much as she could manage to make herself tea and
toast before she had gone to bed the night before.

Hugh had said he would return some time today. At
the thought of his impending presence Leah huddled
back under the duvet. She had an overwhelming desire
to pull it up over her head and stay where she was for
the rest of her life.

Why had she reacted as she had to him? At the
thought of her body's physical response to his touch
she cringed. What on earth had he thought of her? She
barely knew him and yet she had practically offered
herself to him. He had shown quite clearly what he
thought of her though. Any lovemaking on his part had
to be due to purely physical attraction.

Leah should have risen and taken more pain-killers
but the effort was too much. She had skipped lunch the
day before and the toast at the end of the day was
insufficient for her hard physical activity. Now she was
hungry, hurting and mortified. The bed was lumpy and

the window was dirty. Everything she looked at and thought about became another object of misery. There was nothing to get up for. No one cared whether she lived or died, she decided. What on earth was she doing in this God-forsaken hole? By mid-morning she was wallowing in so much self-pity that she was almost enjoying herself.

The sound of a vehicle on the track leading up to the house roused her with a jolt. She sat up and stared out of the window. Hugh. With a most unladylike expletive she dived back under the duvet.

'Go away!' she yelled as Hugh's knock reverberated through the house. 'I don't need anything.'

There was the sound of heavy footsteps on the veranda and, to Leah's horror, Hugh's face appeared at the bedroom window. She had raised it an inch or so for fresh air during the night. In one sweeping movement Hugh had pushed it up to its full height. He stood, framed, before her.

'Are you ill?' he enquired politely. He glanced pointedly at his watch. 'Eleven-thirty. I guess it is early at that. Did I wake you?' he asked solicitously.

'No.' Leah sat up, her duvet pulled up to her chin. 'What do you want?'

He suppressed a smile. 'I thought you might need help getting dressed.'

'No!' It was practically a yelp, and Hugh's smile broadened.

'Suit yourself, lady. I'm actually just here as a delivery boy.'

'What do you mean?' Leah glared at him.

'Don't go away.' He swung himself off the veranda and strode off to his vehicle. A minute later he was back. His hand reached in through the window and a tiny bundle of white fur was deposited on Leah's bed. The lamb.

'Oh!' Leah's misery was forgotten. Her bandaged hands reached out and caught the tiny creature. 'Oh, you gorgeous thing. You've made it.'

'None the worse at all for his adventures,' Hugh agreed benignly. 'He's yours.'

'Mine?'

'That's right. You've got a farm, Leah Craig. What sort of a farm is a farm without animals?'

Leah gazed down with delight at the tiny lamb, then up at the big tanned figure at the window.

'Thank you,' she said seriously. 'It's a lovely, generous gesture. I can't keep him though. You said yourself his place is with his mum.'

'Of course it is,' Hugh agreed equitably. With a sweep of his hand he gestured to his four-wheel-drive vehicle parked below the veranda. A woolly face was peering anxiously out of the window. Her misery forgotten, Leah burst into delighted laughter.

'I don't know the first thing about sheep,' she confessed.

'You don't need to,' Hugh reassured her. 'At least, not for a while.' He motioned towards the overgrown home paddock. 'Feed for the ewe is no problem, there's the river or the dams for water, and Mum will take care of Junior. They can still be part of my flock, so if you've problems or when you decide to pack up traps and take yourself back to the city they can simply come home.'

Leah looked down at the tiny bundle on the bed, then up at the man framed in the window.

'Thank you,' she said simply. Then, 'Why are you doing this for me?'

Hugh reached in and scooped up the nervous little creature on the bed. 'Don't look a gift horse in the mouth, Leah Craig.'

'Beware of Scots bearing gifts,' Leah said with asperity, and Hugh grinned.

'Wrong country, ma'am. Not that it's not a lot more apt than the original version. Tell you what. Get yourself respectable, I'll settle these two into their new home and I'll meet you in the kitchen in ten minutes.'

Leah didn't reply for a moment. She was trying to decide what she should do. Did she really want this man in the house with her after what had happened the night before? As if reading her thoughts Hugh reached in and touched her cheek lightly.

'Don't panic. I'm not going to rape you, Dr Craig. Let's agree that what occurred last night was a moment of pure madness and forget it ever happened. If you could manage to cover your body up, I'll make every attempt to forget you're a woman. It's as a doctor I want to talk to you.'

'There are three of me though, aren't there?' Leah asked quietly. 'The woman, the doctor and the heir to this farm.'

Hugh's mouth tightened. 'Well, we'll forget that too. As I said, I want to talk to the doctor.'

'Fine,' Leah said shortly. She reached over and slammed the window shut.

Ten minutes later she had clumsily dressed and run a brush through her hair. Bandaged, her hands were able to do most things, even if it did take three times as long as usual to do them. She washed her face by the simple expedient of running a basin full of cold water and immersing her whole face. Make-up was abandoned; it was simply too difficult.

Hugh was waiting for her as she emerged from the bathroom. The kettle was already on the stove and he was delving into the ancient refrigerator.

'Eggs and bacon?' he asked. 'You seem to be very well stocked.' He located a big frying-pan and returned to the stove.

'How did you get in?' she demanded. 'The front door was locked.'

For answer he held out a key. 'I've had a key to this place for the past twelve months,' he said seriously. 'When your uncle was ill I made him give me one. The district nurse and I used to use it.'

Leah bit her lip. The old man's lonely death had certainly upset Hugh. Leah felt as if she had been judged and sentenced without a trial. She remembered the only time she had ever met her great-uncle and her mouth tightened. If he'd had a lonely death he had only himself to blame. She realised that Hugh was watching her as he cooked.

'You did know him?' he asked. What was he hoping? Leah thought bitterly. That she could somehow be let off the hook by claiming she had not known of his existence?

'Oh, I knew him,' she said bitterly. 'Now,' she changed the subject implacably, 'what do you want?'

Hugh strode across to the dresser and picked up two plates. 'First, breakfast. Or, to be more precise, your breakfast, my lunch.'

'Aren't you working today?' Leah asked curiously. Hugh sighed.

'In case you haven't noticed, today is Sunday.' He lifted a hand and started raising fingers. 'I have been up since six this morning. I have been around the sheep. I have done a ward round. I have done two house calls and I have sewn up a cut on Johnny Ray's leg. I have been home and fetched Dora and son——' he motioned out to the paddock in front of the house where the ewe and her lamb were investigating their new home '—and now I am ready for lunch.' He gestured to his waist where a receiver was strapped to his belt. 'If no emergency crops up I may well be able to eat it. After all,' he said morosely, 'it is my day off.'

Leah smiled apologetically. 'I'm sorry.'

He returned the smile, placed two loaded plates on the table and two mugs of coffee, then sat down himself.

They ate in silence. It took concentration for Leah to handle the knife and fork. She was aware that Hugh was watching her but he didn't offer to help. There was still a palpable tension between them. Finally she finished and pushed the plate back.

'Thank you. I needed that.'

Hugh stood and reached for the plate, then moved to the sink.

'Leave them,' Leah protested. 'I can do them. I've got rubber gloves which will fit over the dressing.'

Hugh reached across to the bench where the rubber gloves were lying. He flicked them across to her and kept washing. Leah struggled to put the things on. To her fury as she finally got the fingers into the second glove Hugh put down the dishcloth.

'Finished,' he announced with satisfaction. He turned back to Leah. 'Now, why are you putting those on?'

Leah glared at him and he laughed. He caught her shoulders and propelled her out of the door on to the veranda. Despite the rain it was still warm. He pushed her into a cane chair and sank into another. Below them, Dora grazed contentedly, oblivious to the wet, with her lamb nestled securely at her side.

'Nicely domesticated,' Hugh commented. 'I feel like Pa Kettle.'

'You need about twelve children,' Leah retorted. Hugh looked across at her. His gaze raked her appraisingly from her bare feet to her free-flowing hair. To her fury Leah felt herself blushing a fierce crimson.

'No,' he finally announced. 'You won't do as Ma. You'll have to be one of the kids. You haven't got the bosom.'

'You'll have to proposition Mrs Ross.' Leah smiled. 'She'd make you a lovely Ma.'

'So she would,' Hugh agreed slowly. He shook his head. 'Thank you, Dr Craig. The lady of my dreams has been under my nose all this time and I hadn't even noticed. Mind,' he said reflectively, 'there is the slight problem of Walter.'

'Walter?'

'Walter Ross.' He smiled. 'Mrs Ross's husband of thirty-odd years.'

Leah returned his smile and then quickly turned away. What was it about those deep blue eyes that made her heart turn over? She looked down at her feet in dismay.

'What did you want?' she asked shortly.

There was a long moment of silence. Hugh settled back in his chair and gazed down to the river through the rain.

'Why are you here?' he asked finally. 'Are you having a holiday, or is it something more permanent? I've seen lights on up here for over a week now, and by the look of the place you're not intending to pack up and take off this afternoon.'

'I'm here for a while,' Leah said tightly.

'Why?'

'I don't see that it's any of your business.'

Hugh nodded. 'Neither it is.' He rose and moved to lean against a veranda post. 'Only if there's another doctor in the valley and it looks like it might be long-term I'd like to hear about it.' He was watching her as he talked.

'Why?' Leah sounded ungracious and she knew it, but she was past caring what this man thought of her.

'Because I'm up to my ears in work,' Hugh responded. 'There's no other doctor for thirty miles. House calls are ten miles apart and the locals refuse to go anywhere else when they're sick.' He hesitated. 'The rationale for this place being a one-doctor town is that any really ill patients go to the city. That works for people like Wilf Harvey, who had no intention of dying, but in fact most of my really ill patients are very old. If they went to the city they might have a margin-ally better chance of recovery but most of them don't see that it's worth it. They want to be here, where they've lived out their lives, where their cronies can come and visit them and where they've known most of the staff for years. I can understand their reasoning but it means more and more that I'm taking on cases I'm not really set up for.'

'So?'

He smiled. 'I'm not complaining.' He looked down at Dora and the lamb. 'This was the life I moved here for and I love it. Only it does present some problems.'

'Such as?'

'Such as never being able to get away.' He came back and sat down beside her. 'I've got an elderly heart patient in hospital at the moment. He could suffer another heart attack at any minute.' He motioned to the receiver on his belt. 'I try not to be any more than fifteen minutes away but occasionally even I want some time time off. Plus,' he went on reflectively, 'I would love to be able to do minor surgery here, and for that I have to have an anaesthetist.'

Leah met his eyes directly. 'I knew I was right,' she said. 'Beware of Scots bearing gifts.'

'Why are you here?' he asked again.

Leah looked down at her bandaged hands. Why was she here? To enable her to find the courage to take the type of job Hugh Kendall seemed to be offering?

With him, though? With a man who had already judged her and found her wanting? She grimaced. Still, she intended to stay on the farm for a while. Despite the misery of the morning it felt good, indescribably good after so many years of being rootless, to live in a place that belonged to her.

'I have resigned from radiology,' she said quietly. 'You were right. It wasn't really what I wanted to do. I'm here to think about what I do want out of life.'

'And the boyfriend?'

'Now that,' she said firmly, 'really is none of your business. Am I to take it you're here to offer me a job, Dr Kendall?'

He reached out and touched her hands lightly. 'For the next week or so you're going to be a patient rather than a doctor,' he smiled, 'but yes. I've had approval from the board for the past six months or so to employ another doctor. The only problem is that no doctor in his right mind would want to come to Carslake.'

'Except Dr Hugh Kendall.'

He nodded. 'And perhaps, for some reason I have

yet to fathom, Dr Leah Craig?' His eyebrows asked the question.

Leah nodded slowly. 'Perhaps. As you say, I've at least a week of being useless and I do want some time to get this place into order. Perhaps I could contact you in ten days or so and let you know what I've decided.'

Hugh rose and stood, watching her appraisingly. 'You do that, Dr Craig.' He hesitated. 'Meanwhile you could give me a ring if you need any help before then.' He reached into a pocket and produced a small white card with a hospital and home number.

Leah also rose. 'I don't think I'll need to, thanks,' she said formally. 'I'm sure you'd really rather not help a money-grubbing little heiress more than you need.' She took a deep breath. 'You can take Dora and the lamb back too,' she said firmly. 'Any decision I make will be made because it's what I want to do, not because of a bribe.'

Hugh smiled, refusing to hear the taunt. 'If you must know, Dora has been a pain in the neck for years now. Firstly, she was raised by the previous owner as a pet lamb and thinks she's human. Secondly, the reason she was down near the river when she lambed was that she spends her life staring morosely at this side. She's obviously decided the grass is greener over here. I'm hoping that by letting her come she'll get lonely and come back content with being one of the flock.'

'Doesn't she like the other sheep?'

'Not much.'

'Like master, like sheep,' Leah commented.

'You mean I'm a loner too?'

'It looks that way to me,' Leah replied. 'There are few places less medically isolated than Carslake.'

'Well, perhaps I've done my time of being in the medical mainstream.' He swung off the veranda. 'And perhaps I found that an even more isolated existence.'

Before Leah could reply the sound of a car pulling into the drive made them pause and turn. It was a gleaming silver Mercedes. Warwick.

This weekend had been long enough, thought Leah bitterly. She sighed. She had hoped that Warwick would just accept her note and let things be. She might have known he could do no such thing. It wasn't that he loved her, she was sure. If Warwick had decided to end the relationship a note would have been fine. The problem though was that Leah had taken the initiative.

'I'll go,' Hugh was saying shortly. 'I wouldn't want to spoil your fun.' He climbed into the seat of his battered vehicle and roared noisily off, veering sharply to avoid the approaching car. Leah sat down again on the cane chair and waited for Warwick.

'I can't understand your change of heart,' Warwick was saying for the fifteenth time. 'This time last month you were perfectly contented. We had the whole thing mapped out perfectly.'

'*You* might have,' Leah retorted. 'I don't remember ever being consulted.'

Warwick sighed. He was being very patient. It was Leah who was being difficult.

'Look, Leah, you're just tired and overwrought. Neither of us has really taken a break since we qualified.' He held out his hands to her. 'Tell you what. Why don't we get married and take a full month for a honeymoon? We could go somewhere really special. How about a month in Europe? I've a couple of clients over there who would really appreciate a personal visit.'

Inwardly Leah cringed. She did a silent count to ten before replying.

'Warwick, please, can we just leave it?' She met his eyes directly. 'We've been really good friends for years now, and I'd like to keep it like that. Can't you see that friends is all we are though?'

'Leah, I need a wife.'

'I know,' she agreed. She had suspected all along that Warwick needed a wife before he could be promoted. 'Warwick, I'd love to oblige but it really isn't a good enough reason to marry.'

'But you love me.' It was a statement of fact and Leah noted his pronouns with detached interest. Not 'I love you' but 'You love me'.

'No,' she said gently. 'I don't. I'm fond of you and until now I've depended on you. It's not enough.'

'It's Kendall, isn't it?' he demanded quietly. Leah shook her head numbly but he persisted. 'You're mad. To give up everything we could have had for this?' He motioned around him with distaste.

'You mean three bathrooms and a tennis court?' Leah queried. Again she shook her head. 'Warwick, I don't need them.'

'You've got your love to keep you warm,' he mocked savagely. 'God help you, then.' He picked up his jacket from where he had flung it across a chair. 'I'll leave you to it. Obviously my presence is not required.'

'Warwick, please,' Leah pleaded. 'Can't we stay as friends?'

He paused at the door and looked back. 'Leah, you've made your choice.' Then suddenly there was a faint glimmer of a smile and a trace of the reason Leah

had stayed friends with this man for so long. 'I wish
you six kids and no washing-machine.'

Leah returned the smile, and went over to kiss him
gently on the cheek. 'And I wish you twelve bathrooms
and a beautiful wife who likes polishing taps.'

Then he was gone, and Leah was left with the surety
that once his pride had been restored with another
more successful relationship she would at least be able
to wish him joy.

It was finished though. Her life as a successful city
doctor was over. What lay ahead must be of her own
making.

CHAPTER SEVEN

THE next few days passed slowly. Leah wandered around the farm with a sense of marking time, waiting for her hands to heal. They refused to oblige. On Thursday her right hand flared into an unrelenting ache. After a sleepless night she woke to a red-hot pain, with insistent throbbing in the deepest of the cuts.

Removing the dressing, she winced at the sight that met her eyes. Angry red lines were leading away from the cut, into her wrist.

She swore softly to herself, dressed and went to sit on the veranda with a cup of coffee. After one sip she put the cup down. It tasted odd. She was feeling distinctly light-headed and, with reluctance, acknowledged that she was running a fever. Dora and Henry, as Leah had now named the lamb, nosed up curiously to greet her.

'What would you do?' Leah demanded, stroking Dora's nose with her good hand. 'It's infected and I need an antibiotic.'

Dora looked up at her with big eyes that told her she understood, and wasn't it just awful? Henry wiggled his tail and applied himself to breakfast.

'I can't drive all the way back to town with my hand like this,' Leah went on grimly. 'Damn. Why don't I keep some antibiotic in my medical bag?'

Dora lay her head on Leah's lap and gave her a sympathetic nudge.

'You're right, of course,' Leah said wearily. 'What use has a radiologist for antibiotics?' She sighed. 'I'm going to have to go to him, aren't I?'

Dora looked up again and Leah nodded. 'OK, if you say so.' She gave Dora a final pat and stood up. 'But it just about chokes me to do it.'

Hugh's surgery was a part of the hospital. Leah parked in front of the low brick building and made her way across to where the sign directed.

The surgery was bright and cheerful, freshly painted with baskets of toys and a huge blackboard running along one wall to keep youngsters amused while waiting. With only one doctor there, waiting would be the order of the day, Leah thought as she made her way to the desk.

'Leah Craig?' The young receptionist took her name with bright interest. 'Aren't you the new doctor?'

Leah shook her head. 'No.' She managed a smile and held out her hands. 'I'm the new patient.'

The girl grinned her response. 'Hi. I'm Rosie.' She looked up at Leah's flushed countenance and back down again at Leah's hands, before gesturing towards one of the comfortably upholstered chairs. 'Take a seat. You shouldn't have to wait any more than about half an hour.'

It was slightly more than that, and by the time Leah was shown into Hugh's room the combination of pain, nausea and nerves was making it hard for her to even rise from her chair. 'You're being silly,' she told herself firmly. 'You're over-reacting to your arm and you're over-reacting to Hugh. He's just a doctor and I'm just a patient.'

It was a nice try but it didn't work. The butterflies

were still there and at the sight of Hugh's tanned countenance behind the desk they started racing around in mad circles. He stood as she entered the room.

'Well. . .' It was a slow exclamation of surprise. 'Dr Craig.' A slow smile started behind his eyes. 'Have you made up your mind already?'

'No, I haven't,' Leah snapped and then bit her lip. She closed her eyes and then started again. 'I'm here as a patient.'

He nodded, for the first time noticing the lines of pain around her eyes. 'Your hands?'

'Yes.'

He came around the desk and pushed her gently into a chair.

'Which one?'

She held up her right hand. She had been forced to use it on the drive to the hospital and it was protesting in no uncertain terms. Even Hugh's touch as he unwound the dressing sent shooting stabs of pain up her arm. He grimaced as he saw it.

'Ouch.' He flicked a sharp, concerned glance up at her. 'This hasn't just happened this morning.'

'It was hurting yesterday,' she admitted. 'I spent the day telling myself it was my imagination.'

'Damn fool,' he said unemotionally. He turned to the bench behind him and loaded a syringe. Leah used her left hand to pull up her shirt sleeve and he plunged the antibiotic into her arm.

'Thanks,' she said briefly. 'Can you give me a script for some oral antibiotic?'

He shook his head. 'No. You're not going home, Leah. Not with your arm like that.' He looked again at the red lines and then gently prodded the glands under her armpit. 'Tender?'

She winced.

'There you are, then,' he said firmly. He pushed a button on his desk and Rosie's bright face appeared. 'Rosie, I want you to take Dr Craig over to Matron.' He picked up the phone. 'I'll let her know what's happening.' He looked at Leah. 'I want you in bed with a drip in your arm within fifteen minutes. You know as well as I do that you stand a very good risk of a massive overall infection with your arm in that state.'

'Can't I go home and get some things?' Leah said helplessly. She knew he was right. She should have come prepared but her mind just hadn't let her accept how serious it was.

'Matron will find a nightie and toothbrush,' Hugh said firmly. 'What else could a girl want?'

'What else indeed?' Leah asked bitterly. Abandoning the argument, she followed Rosie's already retreating back.

Despite her reluctance it was with a sense of relief that she sank on to the crisp white sheets of the hospital bed. Matron, middle-aged and motherly, took one look at Leah's strained face and took control. Leah was undressed by cool, competent hands without having to do anything.

Before she knew it she was in a hospital nightgown and the pain-killer that Hugh had obviously ordered had been administered. By the time he arrived to set up the drip it was starting to work and she was drifting into a hazy sleep.

'That's more like it,' he said approvingly.

She looked up at him through a mist of drug-induced drowsiness. 'Thank you,' she said simply.

He didn't answer, but turned his attention to the drip stand. With it adjusted to his satisfaction he turned back to the bed.

'OK, Dr Craig. We've done our bit. Now you concentrate on recovering.'

Matron smiled and bustled out. For a moment Hugh stood looking down at the bed. His smile faded. From what seemed a long way away Leah watched him, her eyes meeting his. He lifted a hand and ran a finger down her cheek. Momentarily the harsh look disappeared; then, as if catching himself, it returned and he was gone, his footsteps echoing down the corridor as he strode back to meet the demands of the rest of the morning's surgery.

It took two days for Leah to shake the fever, and when she could finally think clearly again she found the infection had left her as weak as a kitten.

The nursing staff were aware of her status as a doctor, and either for that reason or because of her relationship with her great-uncle she was treated with reserve. Matron popped into her room for a chat when she had time, obviously suppressing any reserve she might have felt, but for the rest Leah was left alone.

She saw very little of Hugh. He saw to her immediate medical needs but otherwise stayed well away. As Leah lay in bed she could hear his resonant voice chatting to the other patients as he did his ward rounds. In comparison the time he spent in her room was slight.

She minded. It was stupid, but she was beginning to acknowledge to herself that she minded. This big man with the gentle smile and crinkling blue eyes was beginning to mean more to her than Warwick ever had. He walked into the room and her heart started doing crazy somersaults. When he walked out again after giving curt instructions to the attending nurses she felt like turning her head into the pillow and crying like a baby.

It was because she was ill, she told herself. Her illness was accentuating her aloneness. Surely in normal healthy times he wouldn't have had this effect on her.

By the end of her second day in hospital Leah was as miserable as she had ever been. Her hand hurt, her head ached and she wanted to go home. She knew herself though that she had at least another couple of days to go. Hugh would be negligent if he let her leave before he was certain the infection had cleared.

After dinner, as evening visitors flooded into the other rooms, she turned her face to the wall and abandoned herself to her misery. The sound of the door opening behind her made her close her eyes in distress. She wasn't fit to face the nursing staff.

'Can I come in, dear?'

Leah sniffed, searched for a handkerchief under her pillow and rolled over. It was Mrs Ross, maker of lemon meringue pie supreme.

'There, now,' she clucked as she saw the extent of the ravages to Leah's face. 'If I wasn't saying to Walter you'd be needing a visitor.'

Leah blew her nose fiercely and struggled to sit up. 'I do not need a visitor.'

'No, dear,' her visitor agreed kindly. 'I guess you're just crying because your hand hurts.'

Leah tried to summon up a glare but it didn't quite come off. Mrs Ross would have been oblivious anyway. She was delving into an ample shopping-bag.

'There you go. A nice tin of chocolate-chip cookies I

made myself this afternoon, for if you get hungry in the night.' She placed it on Leah's tray and kept on delving. 'A tin of talc.' She beamed up at Leah. 'I hope you like it. Lily of the Valley. My favourite.' She placed it on top of the biscuits and, with the air of a magician conjuring up a rabbit, produced her last offering. 'Violets. I made Walter pick 'em this afternoon.' She buried her nose into the posy. 'Don't they smell a treat?' She looked up at Leah and smiled.

Leah couldn't respond. Her gaze went from the tins on her tray, to the violets, and then up to the kindly face watching her expectantly. Weak tears started to again slide down the already tear-stained cheeks.

'Now don't you turn into a damp rag with me,' her visitor warned firmly. 'Otherwise I'll take 'em back. Every one.'

Leah smiled through her tears. 'I'm sorry. You mustn't think I'm ungrateful. It's just that you've been so lovely and everyone thinks I'm so awful.'

'What do you mean?'

'Because I didn't visit my great-uncle.' Leah's voice trembled but she plugged on. 'I can't work here. They're all judging me.'

'Now that,' Mrs Ross pronounced, settling herself into Leah's visitor's chair, 'is nonsense. Your treatment of your relations is no one's business except yours. Besides,' she continued reflectively, 'I don't reckon anyone but me 'n' Doc Kendall would know about it. As far as the staff here would know you've bought the farm or are renting or anything. I sure as eggs haven't told anyone and I don't see why Doc Kendall would.'

'Then why don't they talk to me?' Leah wailed.

Mrs Ross shook her head. 'Goodness, you have worked yourself into a nice state, haven't you? And I nearly didn't come in, being unsure as to whether I was wanted. Don't you see what's as plain as the nose on your face?' As Leah shook her head Mrs Ross sighed. 'What is common knowledge around here is that you're a doctor and Doc Kendall is trying to persuade you to work here. If that's not enough to make the junior nurses quiet in front of you, I don't know what is. They'll be so busy watching their Ps and Qs they won't have time to chat.'

'Is that all it is?'

'Have you ever been in hospital since you qualified?' Mrs Ross demanded.

'No.'

'Well, believe me, then.' She smiled. 'Nurses still don't treat doctors as completely human, at least not in these backwoods yet anyway.'

'And Hugh? I mean, Dr Kendall?'

'Well, perhaps he hasn't got all that much time for chatting.' Then, at the sceptical look on Leah's face the lady nodded. 'All right. You may be right there. Doc Kendall was your great-uncle's closest neighbour as well as his doctor. I know he was pretty concerned with how alone the old man was. It would have come as a shock to him to hear of your existence after the old man died.'

Leah lay back on the pillows and stared at the ceiling. The old bitterness welled up. He had the power to hurt her even yet.

'Would you like to hear my side of the story?' she asked softly.

The woman on the chair beside the bed watched her with sympathetic eyes. 'I don't need to,' she said firmly. 'I'm no longer judging you. I know there's got to be a reason. But if you'd like to tell it, then I'm listening.'

Leah started hesitantly. 'I was thirteen when my parents were killed in a car smash,' she said quietly. 'I was an only child. There wasn't much money and, without my parents, I had no relatives other than my great-uncle. Howard Reece. I didn't know him. I'd heard my father talk about him and knew they didn't get on. I had to stay in a home while they tried to work out what to do with me. I was too shocked to think for a while, but finally I remembered my great-uncle.'

Leah hesitated, remembering back to the scene that had ensued. Beside her Mrs Ross sat in silence, sensing Leah's need to talk.

'The social welfare people were relieved,' she went on. 'Foster parents for thirteen-year-old girls are almost impossible to find. The social worker assigned to me wrote to my uncle and, when she didn't hear back, brought me to Carslake to see him.'

This time the silence was so long that Mrs Ross stirred. 'Well?'

Leah gave a bitter little laugh. 'That's really the end of the story.' She grimaced and took a deep breath. 'The first thing he wanted to know was whether there was any money. When the social worker told him my parents had died with very little he turned on her and accused her of trying to foist a "social welfare brat" on to him and to get off his land.'

'Oh, my dear.'

Leah shook her head. 'Don't be sorry,' she said softly. 'I got by and I was lucky. They did manage to keep me in foster homes. A couple of them were quite good. I managed to win a scholarship which saw me through medicine, and here I am.'

'You never saw Howard Reece again?'

'No.' Leah's voice was clearer now, as if by talking

about it she had purged the worst of the memories. 'I only ever tried to contact him once after that.'

'When was that?'

'At my graduation.' Leah thought back to the huge celebration. She had been friends with Warwick by then and was organised to be part of an enormous group of his parents, aunts and uncles, grandparents and brothers and sisters. As her own tiny gesture to the event she had written a letter to Howard Reece, inviting him to be part of it. He had never replied.

'The old goat.' Mrs Ross's eyes were like flint. 'And to think I used to feel so sorry for him.'

'Perhaps you were right,' Leah said reflectively. 'Just because he caused himself to be so isolated, it doesn't mean you can't feel sorry for him.' She stirred on the bed and shifted her aching arm. 'After those rebuffs I couldn't make another effort, though perhaps if I'd known he needed me as I needed him all those years ago I could have tried.'

'Well!' It was an expletive of anger. 'And to think here's Doc Kendall thinking you're a heartless little baggage.' She stood up and picked up her basket. 'I'll soon put that right.'

'No!' Leah sat up sharply, jolting her arm in the process. She winced. 'You're not to tell him.'

'But——'

'No,' Leah said firmly. 'I don't want anyone making my excuses to Hugh Kendall for me. If he wants to judge something he knows nothing about then it's up to him.'

'But, dear, that's crazy.'

'I don't care.' The thought of Hugh Kendall feeling sorry for her was suddenly more than she could bear. 'You promise?'

Mrs Ross sighed. 'Very well, dear, but I think you're making a mistake. Now, when are you getting out of here?'

Leah looked up to the drip above her bed. 'Not for a couple of days, I guess.'

'Would you like your own nighties?'

Leah grinned. 'I would kill for my own nighties.' She surveyed the shapeless hospital gown with distaste.

'It's not much out of my way to drop in to your place on the way home and pick up what you want. Make a list and give me a key.'

When Mrs Ross had left the gloom of the past few days left with her. Whether it was her cheerful company or whether it was just the opportunity to talk, Leah didn't know. All at once the cloud of oppression was lifted. Even her arm didn't hurt so much.

When a nurse came in, doing temperature and blood-pressure, silent and efficient, Leah was even able to summon a big smile and start chatting. To her delight, after a startled look, the girl responded. Mrs Ross was right. It was wariness rather than coldness that had kept the nursing staff at bay.

Later that night Hugh came in. He surveyed her chart with satisfaction.

'Good. We can discontinue the drip, I think.'

'Hooray,' Leah said thankfully. 'Home on Tuesday?'

'I don't see why not.' He smiled down at her. 'As long as you don't engage in any strenuous or grubby activities.'

'Scout's honour,' she said solemnly, and he laughed. As he turned to go she stopped him. 'Hugh?'

'Yes?'

'Can I start work on Monday week?'

He turned back to the bed. 'Do you really want to?'

'I guess it depends what you've got for me,' she said seriously. 'But if you can keep me busy then I'm available.'

'If I can keep you busy?' He whistled. 'How about five sessions of clinic a week, assistance with theatre on two afternoons and for emergencies and general back-up?'

She stared. 'As much as that? That's a full-time load!'

He nodded. 'We've got patients who are travelling thirty miles to see a doctor because they can't get in to see me.'

'It only took three quarters of an hour to see me on Friday,' she said, puzzled.

'That's because you came in as an urgent case.' he explained. 'I always try to leave some room for people needing immediate care or who can't travel. If you'd rung up looking for an appointment for an ingrown toenail you'd have been given an appointment next Thursday fortnight.'

'As bad at that?'

'As bad as that.'

'No wonder you're prepared to take me on.'

He gave her a long look. 'I have the impression that you're an exceedingly competent doctor, Dr Craig. I wouldn't be taking you on otherwise.'

'Despite what you think of me personally.'

The look intensified. There was a long silence before Hugh finally broke it.

'As you say,' he said quietly before turning to leave the room.

Leah used the next twenty-four hours to familiarise herself with the hospital. Respectably clad again in her own nightwear, courtesy of Mrs Ross's generosity, she investigated the building and made an attempt to get to know all the staff.

Once her own wariness had worn off the staff responded to her with friendly helpfulness. They were clearly delighted at the thought of another doctor on the staff.

'It's going to make the hospital busier,' Leah warned. 'If Hugh and I start doing elective surgery that's the end of your empty beds.'

'That's the way we like it,' Matron said firmly. 'If I'm going to nurse, then that's what I want to do. Besides,' she went on severely, 'there's too much knitting on night duty for my liking. It'll do the staff good to earn their keep for a change.'

On Monday afternoon Leah dressed and, with Hugh's permission, took a quiet stroll down to the town. It felt odd to be out of the hospital; strangely unreal. That's only after four days, she thought in surprise, trying to imagine how difficult it must be to adjust to a stay of some weeks.

Carslake itself was a tiny service centre. Up the road from the hospital was a general store, a petrol station, a pub and a school. The town looked out of place against its wild setting. Were the people to move out tomorrow the bush would reclaim the place within twelve months.

As she walked Leah was greeted by the locals in terms that showed without doubt they knew she was the new doctor. In a town this size it would be impossible to be anonymous.

Tired after only half an hour or so, she retraced her steps to the long, low hospital building at the end of the main road. As she slipped gratefully back into her newly made bed she thought of the comparison

between her old job at City Central and her new job at
Carslake. The medical environments were worlds
apart. She fell to sleep wondering how on earth she
could have made such a mad decision.

CHAPTER EIGHT

LEAH's first few weeks in her new job were a confused blur. She had thought she was a qualified doctor; in those weeks it seemed as if she had known nothing. General practice was a world away from the medicine of City Central.

At the end of the first week Leah thought she had made a horrible mistake. At the end of a month she was fairly sure she had made the right decision.

Her clinics were a joy. From an environment at City Central where she was discouraged from taking a personal interest in patients, here it was what the job was all about. Leah discovered that three quarters of her job was listening—about ills real and imagined, and sometimes to fears and worries that were totally unrelated to medicine.

Leah settled back and listened. There was little else she could do to start with as all her patients were new to her, but in many cases she found that listening was all that was required.

There was enough real medicine to keep her on her toes. The common illnesses and accidents of a rural community presented themselves in a never-ending stream.

Twice a week she and Hugh operated, and here Leah was at her most certain that she had done the right thing. Hugh's skill as a surgeon far surpassed what was usual in a general practitioner and Leah took real pleasure in watching and learning as she administered anaesthetics. She had done a rotating period of anaesthetics at City Central during her residency, for which she was now profoundly grateful.

'What's Hugh's background?' she asked Mrs Ross one morning. Leah had come in early to check on a patient in the first stages of labour, and was now sitting over her third cup of coffee of the morning in Mrs Ross's kitchen.

'You shouldn't drink so much of that stuff,' the cook said firmly. 'It'll addle your insides.'

'My insides were addled years ago,' Leah said placidly. 'Are you changing the subject?'

'Nope.' Mrs Ross emptied a basin of scone dough out on to the bench and started the task of rolling and cutting. 'I don't know very much. Why don't you ask him?'

'I daren't.' Leah grimaced. 'I'm scared he'll tell me it's none of my business.'

'And neither it is, young lady,' the cook chuckled. 'Do you want some breakfast?'

'I don't believe in it.'

Mrs Ross shook her head sadly. 'The younger generation! I don't know what's going to become of them.'

'We'll survive,' Leah said sagely. 'Especially if you keep feeding us on scones with jam and cream for morning tea.' She glanced at her watch. 'I'd better go. Isn't there any gossip in this hospital about Hugh Kendall?'

'Not that I've heard, and I've been listening all the time.'

Leah whirled, turning bright crimson as she did so. Hugh stood framed in the doorway.

'Oops.' The situation was irretrievable and she knew it. She sought for composure. 'Sorry,' she made herself say, then smiled. 'You really shouldn't creep up on ladies unawares.'

He smiled too and the tension broke. 'I'm not creeping. I'm searching for some toast.'

'A sensible man,' Mrs Ross approved. 'You sit yourself down and I'll find a strip or two of bacon to go with it.'

'You could wait for staff breakfast,' Leah said with asperity.

Hugh glanced at his watch. 'That's not for three quarters of an hour. I want to get home and go around the sheep before morning surgery.'

'Were you called out?' Leah and Hugh had developed a system where she did the night calls back to the hospital and Hugh did the night house calls. They were almost equal in frequency but the thought of driving around unknown countryside at night looking for addresses of patients she didn't know left Leah cold. Country practice had its drawbacks.

Hugh nodded. 'A gall bladder. His wife's bringing him in. And you?'

'Mrs Robinson's in labour. At least,' she corrected herself, 'Mrs Robinson *thinks* she's in labour. Personally I can't find any evidence of it.'

'Does she want me?' Midwifery patients were given the choice of staying with Hugh. As he'd looked after them for their entire pregnancies it would have been unfair for them to have to change doctors at delivery.

'She doesn't mind.' Leah smiled. 'The way she's going, by the time she delivers the babe we'll be old friends.' She put down her coffee-cup and stood up resolutely. 'I'll leave you to it. I want to go home, shower, and check my sheep too.'

'The whole two of them,' Hugh mocked.

'It's a big responsibility,' Leah said gravely.

It was working out better than she had expected, Leah thought as she drove home through the early-morning mist. Between her and Hugh there existed a fine current of tension of which she was always aware. Hugh, however, was unfailingly pleasant and courteous. Both of them were working hard to establish a solid medical partnership. Their skills blended and complemented each other. They were already finding that the patients were segregating painlessly to prefer either Hugh's blunt approach or Leah's sympathetic listening.

The mist lifted and the morning sun broke through as Leah turned into her farm's gate. Below the level of the road, the derelict little farmhouse looked picturesque and quaint, with Dora and Henry rousing themselves lazily to check the intrusion of the car engine into their solitude. Leah had an overwhelming sense of peace and satisfaction.

If only she could find some way of being at ease with Hugh. Since the day they had met she had been on edge. She looked across the valley towards his land. A wisp of smoke floated lazily upwards, giving the only sign of human habitation. Soon he would be home, checking his flocks for trouble and setting his farm in order before his day's work.

Leah's loneliness descended again like a cloud. She felt an almost unbearable longing to be on the other side of the river, at a farmhouse which wasn't hers. She thought back to the companionship of the hospital kitchen, Mrs Ross's friendliness and Hugh. . .

Hugh. It was Hugh she wanted to be with, she

acknowledged to herself, and the knowledge flooded through her with absolute certainty. Despite what he thought of her, she was in love with Hugh Kendall.

So now what? Leah mechanically showered and readied herself for her day's work. She glanced at her watch as she put the final touches to her make-up. It almost seemed trivial to bother with make-up in this job, she thought. For night calls there was often little time to do more than run a perfunctory comb through her hair. The patients, the nursing staff and Hugh saw her as nature intended. Given time however she enjoyed taking pains with her appearance.

And why? she asked herself. For Hugh?

Damn him. She banged the hairbrush heavily on the dresser, and found herself irretrievably drawn to the window. Across the river the wisp of smoke still floated lazily upwards. It was a tangible link with the man on the other side of the valley.

She had work to do. In hard work lay the only course through the minefield of emotion surrounding her. She had a full surgery booked today, she had three of her own patients in hospital, she had promised to do a house call on old Mrs Rawlins, and Mrs Robinson was bound to deliver just as the day reached its busiest. She might be in love but there was no time to stay staring out of windows like a moonstruck teenager.

The day proved to be busier even than Leah had expected. It was Friday and there was always a rush as people realised that normal surgery would not be on again until Monday. The only thing which didn't eventuate was Mrs Robinson's baby, and Leah went to sleep that night expecting to be woken.

She slept lightly but no call came. On Saturday morning Leah set up a drip to hurry the labour along.

Things had been niggling for long enough. After thirty-six hours of irregular contractions the girl was becoming distraught.

'Do I need a Caesarian?' she asked fearfully as Leah set up the drip.

Leah shook her head and smiled down at the worried mother-to-be.

'No. There's no indication that there's anything wrong at all. This baby's taking its own sweet time. The only reason I'm trying to hurry things up is because you're getting tired.' She looked over at the expectant father, who looked almost more haggard than his wife. 'The only way any of us are going to get any sleep tonight is if I can persuade Junior to get a move on.'

Still it dragged on and, as the afternoon passed, Leah became more and more concerned. Should she have performed a Caesarian? It was getting to be past the point of no return now. Had she made the right decision?

It was at this stage that during her residency Leah would have called in the consultant obstetrician. Who was there here? Hugh. She bit her lip ruefully. The man had no specialist obstetric skills.

The thought of being completely on her own finally drove her to the phone. Leah had never been in the situation of having no specialist back-up and she wasn't enjoying the sensation.

Hugh answered immediately and Leah could imagine him grimacing as his peaceful afternoon on the farm was interrupted. Less than ten minutes after her phone call, however, she heard his increasingly familiar stride in the corridor.

No matter how long she stayed in medicine she could never develop the aura that Hugh Kendall had, Leah thought bitterly. He walked into a room and patients relaxed. Even she found herself with a lessening of tension as he performed his own examination.

The tension didn't lessen for long. Despite full dilation the baby was staying stubbornly in mid-cavity. As Hugh finished his examination a trace of meconium appeared, the first sign of foetal distress.

By the time a local anaesthetic had been administered the signs of foetal distress were becoming clearer. The pulse rate had dropped, from a healthy hundred and forty ten minutes ago to a worrying sixty. Leah sent up a silent prayer of thankfulness that she had not delayed asking for help any longer.

As it was, with the baby distressed and its head still high, Leah was in a situation where she would have given a lot to be back at City Central. She wanted a trained obstetrician and paediatrician, with all the associated sophisticated equipment at their disposal. All she had was Hugh Kendall.

The problem with obstetrics was that no one could ever predict that there was likely to be a problem, Leah thought grimly. Things could go wrong so fast. Such as now. She was moving swiftly, assisting Hugh to prepare for a forceps delivery and thinking all the time, Why didn't I do a Caesarian? To lose the baby now. . .

It wasn't going to happen. In one swift movement the forceps were in use. Hugh gently applied pressure, feeling the resistance as he waited for the next contraction. As it came he applied pressure in earnest. He eased off slightly as the contraction passed and the head was in view. Leah found herself holding her breath. The length between contractions was interminable.

In reality it was seconds. Within a minute Hugh was clearing the airway of the newly delivered baby girl.

Her first sound was like that of a new-born kitten. Leah looked up in concern from where she had moved to in order to take over the care of the exhausted mother. While she watched the baby seemed to come to a decision. Her little lungs heaved, she opened her mouth and wailed.

'I should have given her a Caesar,' Leah said ruefully as they left the room together. 'If you hadn't been here I would have lost the baby.'

Hugh shook his head. 'It's so hard to know,' he said sympathetically. 'Should you give a woman a Caesar because she's getting tired? Lots of doctors do, and perform lots of unnecessary Caesarians because of it. Mrs Robinson will be grateful that you didn't.'

'And yet I nearly lost her baby.'

'No. You weren't to anticipate those final problems. Besides which, if I hadn't been here I wouldn't mind betting that you'd have got that baby out alive. It's amazing the skills that desperation can teach.'

'So where did you learn your obstetric skills?' Leah demanded. 'You handle forceps like an obstetrician with ten years' experience.'

'Well, perhaps I've had that,' he said quietly.

Leah did a quick calculation in her head. It didn't need a mathematical degree to tell her the thing was impossible.

'You can't be more than thirty-five,' she said accusingly. 'You've obviously done a fair stint at surgery and an equal amount of training in obstetrics. And yet here you are being a GP in as remote an area of the world as you'd ever be likely to find.'

'There are more remote areas.'

'Such as?'

'Try the outlying areas of Ethiopia and see if you can find a City Central hospital with a fully equipped obstetric team.'

'Is that where you've been?' Leah asked curiously.

He nodded. 'Until two years ago.'

'And the surgical and obstetric experience?'

'All learned on the job.' They were walking towards the car park as they spoke. 'Out there you don't see many nervous headaches or kids with a three-hour-old tummy ache. Every patient who's managed to find their way to the hospital is sick. All the births we dealt with were complicated. The straightforward deliveries never came near us. And, as I said, it's amazing the skills that desperation can teach.' He paused, then added reflectively, 'The awful thing was that by the time the woman sought help it was nearly always too late—at least for the baby.'

'And your surgical experience?'

'The same. We had one fully qualified surgeon on the team but he couldn't stretch himself far enough. When it was hot we were all called in.'

'Hot?'

'When the camps were bombed. Or when we got a truck-load of soldiers. We weren't supposed to deal with military medical matters but often it was a case of us or no one.'

Leah was silent. They had stopped by her truck. 'So how did you end up here?' she finally asked.

'I was in Ethiopia for five years,' Hugh said softly. 'After those five years I felt older than I ever want to feel again.'

He frowned and changed the subject.

'What are you doing with yourself for the rest of the afternoon, Dr Craig?'

Leah glanced at her watch. Three o'clock. The rest of the afternoon stretched before her.

'I don't know,' she confessed. 'Go home and catch up on a little sleep, I guess. I lay awake waiting for the hospital to ring for Mrs Robinson all last night.'

'More fool you,' Hugh said unsympathetically. 'The sign of a very young doctor is one who lies awake hoping for the phone to ring.' He smiled his slow, pulse-quickening smile that made Leah's heart swell within her. 'Tell you what—what about learning some practical farming? I'm going home to mark the lambs. Get some old clothes and sturdy boots on and come over and give me a hand.'

'OK,' Leah agreed cautiously. She wasn't sure that she was being wise. The way her body reacted to this man she should simply walk away from this place and never return. She gave herself a mental shake. Surely what she was feeling was some sort of purely physical reaction? Perhaps she needed to spend more time near Hugh Kendall in order to overcome it. Perhaps she was just kidding herself. . .

Half an hour later her little utility truck swung into Hugh's drive. His house was a neater version of hers, newly painted with a carefully tended cottage garden surrounding it. The man must be a workaholic, Leah thought in dismay.

There was a call from below the house and Leah looked down to the mustering yards. A group of lambs were penned. From the other side of the fence their mothers bleated dismally.

Hugh motioned towards a rail beside the yard.

'There's your equipment. Come over and I'll show you what to do.'

Leah picked up the knife on the rail, turned it over and looked at Hugh in horror.

'What on earth are you doing?'

'Marking the lambs,' Hugh said patiently. 'Watch.' He seized another little animal. In seconds the surgical procedure had been completed.

'I thought you meant marking them.' Leah's voice was practically a squeak. 'You know. Writing your name on them or something.'

Hugh grinned. 'No, Dr Craig. I meant marking them. Now are you here to help or not?'

Leah took a deep breath. Hugh was watching her, amusement at her predicament clearly written on his face. It was clear he was expecting her to turn tail and run.

'Show me what to do,' Leah said savagely. 'You want me to mark lambs, I'll mark lambs.'

She watched Hugh do three, until she was quite sure she knew what to do.

'The trick is to work fast,' Hugh explained. 'It's like the old way of pulling out a tooth by tying a string to the door handle. It only works if you've got the courage to do it fast.'

'I've got the picture,' Leah said grimly.

An hour later they were done. Leah walked back to the farmhouse silently. She was sure the man beside her was enjoying himself hugely at her expense.

'Come in and clean up and have a cup of tea,' Hugh suggested.

'No, thank you.' Leah's tone was brusque.

'Leah?'

'Yes?' She didn't look at him.

'Thank you for helping.'

'I'm sure you enjoyed it enormously.' Her tone was bitter.

'I always enjoy passing on knowledge,' Hugh said blandly. 'Who knows, Dr Craig? This time next year you might be marking your own lambs.'

'I think I've decided to go in for beef cattle,' Leah said cautiously, and Hugh gave a shout of laughter.

'Unless you want a herd of belligerent bulls, I've got news for you, Dr Craig. The procedure is exactly the same; just messier.'

Despite herself Leah smiled. 'Pigs, then.'

'They get fleas. Besides, Dr Craig, if you think you can muck out sties in between medical calls you'll soon find yourself with a very small practice. The population of Carslake has some notion of medical nicety. Now, do you really mean to refuse my cup of tea?'

Leah sighed and looked up at the man at her side. 'Why are you offering it?'

Hugh raised his eyebrows. 'Why the suspicion?'

'Because I'm learning very fast that there is always a motive, Dr Kendall.'

He turned and looked at her. His eyes held a glimmer of doubt.

'You want to know why I'm asking you to stay for a while?'

'Yes. I know perfectly well why you asked me to help mark the lambs. I want to know what I'm letting myself in for.'

'A cup of tea and a chance for you to get to know your medical colleague, Dr Craig. Nothing more.'

'Promise?'

'Promise.'

* * *

'OK,' Leah said directly. They were stretched out under a huge gum-tree beside the house, drinking tea out of big porcelain mugs. Below them the land stretched down to the river. Dotted in the paddock were scores of reunited ewes and lambs. An occasional bleat broke the stillness as the lambs expressed their indignation to their mums. Leah hugged her warm mug and gazed pensively down to the water below.

'If this is an opportunity for me to get to know my medical colleague, then fire away,' she demanded.

'What do you mean?' Hugh was stretched out on his back beside her, gazing upwards through the canopy of leaves to the brilliance of the sky above. His voice was slurred with sleepiness.

'Hugh Kendall, if you intend to go to sleep I'm off,' Leah said indignantly. 'You promised to tell me about yourself.'

'I did no such thing.'

'You did.'

'I said you could get to know me. Surely the opportunity to discover whether I snore or not is information enough.'

Leah smiled. For a moment she said nothing. The warmth of the day added to the two nights of broken sleep were beginning to affect her too. There was nothing her body would have liked better than to lie on this bed of grass and sleep the rest of the afternoon away. Especially, she admitted to herself, curled up beside this large male body. She caught herself. 'Tell me,' she said with determination.

'Tell you what?'

'Well, for a start, what made you go to Ethiopia?'

'Lots of things.'

'There's a comprehensive answer.'

'It's a hard question.'

'So how old were you when you went?'

He thought. 'Twenty-eight.'

'So you practised for a while in Edinburgh.'

'Yes.'

Leah gazed down at him thoughtfully. Her questions were an impertinence, but somehow what had already passed between them allowed her to continue. This man hadn't hesitated to offend her. Now it was her turn.

'General practice?' she demanded.

'I did my first part of surgery,' he admitted.

'You didn't enjoy it?'

'I think I enjoyed it very much,' he said quietly.

'So why didn't you finish?'

Hugh looked up at her. 'What is this? The Inquisition?'

Leah looked down at him consideringly. 'Dr Kendall, you know all about me. You know that I'm a heartless little baggage who doesn't give a straw for her relations. You know that I've a boyfriend who drives a Mercedes, who dislikes you intensely and who, in fact, can be almost as rude as you. You know that I'm all wrong for radiology and make a lousy farmer. You've summed me up and judged me nicely. Allow me to do the same to you.' She glared down at him and he smiled.

'Fair enough.'

'Well?'

For a moment she thought he wasn't going to answer. He put his hands behind his head to form a pillow and closed his eyes. When he finally started to talk his voice sounded as if it came from a long way away.

'It was always assumed I would do medicine. I come

from a medical family. My father is a professor of nuclear medicine, my mother is an ophthalmologist. Both of them are at the top of their fields. I have two brothers, both of whom are doing very well in their chosen specialities. For me it was never a matter of whether I did medicine or not, it was a matter of which speciality I'd undertake.'

'So why did you choose surgery?'

'I don't know really.' His voice was still slurred with sleep. 'For all the wrong reasons, I think. I was good at it and it met with general approval. Even at that stage I toyed with the idea of general practice, but in the circles I moved in the words were almost a slur. General practice was something you did if you didn't have the brains to do anything else.'

Leah nodded. It was an attitude rife among the brightest of the medical graduates.

'So what made you change your mind?'

'Time,' Hugh said seriously. 'And maturity. The more I operated the more frustrated I felt at never knowing the patient's full background. The GPs used to come in to visit my surgical patients. I'd see the rappport they'd developed with them and wish that I had time to develop the same kind of relationship. I'd operate on an old lady and remove a tumour, then never hear of her again. Twelve months later I'd find out by accident that she'd died of secondaries.'

'Was that enough to make you abandon surgery?'

'It was enough,' he said softly. 'Although it took one really nasty case to make me see the light.'

'Which was?'

'A child.' Hugh hesitated. When he spoke Leah could still hear the pain from years before in his voice. 'A little boy. He came in with a ruptured spleen. It took me and the surgeon in charge of my unit at the time the best part of a day to save him.'

'But you did save him?'

'Oh, yes.' Hugh's voice was bitter. 'We did a wonderful job.'

'So?' Leah asked curiously.

'I was in charge of him post-operatively.' Hugh hesitated and then continued. 'He'd been abused. He had bruises all over him and, despite what the parents said, I was sure the spleen had been ruptured by a kick.'

'Did you intervene?'

'I tried to.' Hugh's voice was harsh with remembrance of a battle lost. 'I contacted every social welfare agency I could think of. Everywhere I was hit with the same block. The general practitioner in charge of the case knew the family and was sure that their version of the accident was the truth.'

'And you were sure it wasn't.'

'I was sure. The parents had money, influence and could lie through their teeth. The GP was too damn stupid to see past their respectable appearance to the violence that lay beneath.'

'So you had to send him home.'

'I had no choice. I sent him home. Six months later he was dead with a haemorrhage caused by a fractured skull.' He paused, then continued. 'When I heard that, it was as if something inside me snapped. I didn't want to be an outsider any more. I wanted to be in at the grass roots level. If I'd been that child's GP he'd be alive today.'

'You wouldn't have been his doctor, though,' Leah said decisively. 'People like that are always very careful to choose a doctor who's not likely to question their version of events.'

'Maybe,' Hugh said roughly. 'Anyway, at least I have the chance to be involved at that level.'

'And Ethiopia?' Leah asked quietly. There was more behind this man's bitterness than one abused patient.

Hugh smiled wearily. 'It was a natural progression. When I announced I was abandoning surgery my family reacted as if I was out of my mind.'

'All of them?'

'All of them,' Hugh said bitterly. 'Even my fiancée.'

'Fiancée?' Leah asked cautiously.

'The lovely Jane.' Hugh grimaced. 'Jane was well on the way to becoming a highly thought-of radiologist. She had her career mapped out carefully in front of her. I was included in it. Mind you,' he continued reflectively, 'I think my career was expected to follow the same upward curve as hers.'

'She didn't fancy being married to a general practitioner?'

Hugh laughed joylessly. 'General practice, according to Jane, was something akin to leprosy.' He reached down and pulled off a piece of grass, then started stripping it into tiny pieces. 'And you know what the whole damn reasoning was? In every conversation I had the talk came back to money. How much did I expect to earn as a GP? How was I going to support Jane if she took time off to have children? We wouldn't be able to live in the best part of town, the biggest house, as it was always assumed we would do.'

'You couldn't afford three bathrooms?' Leah asked before she could stop herself. A conversation with Warwick swung in the back of her mind.

'No,' Hugh said roughly. 'Only two in the second-best part of town and you'd think I was asking Jane to live in squalor. And I was considered a bastard. My parents, Jane's parents and our friends all thought I was being totally unreasonable. In the end I'd had enough. I contacted an agency for aid abroad, packed my bags and departed.'

'Do you regret it?' Leah asked.

'No.' He closed his eyes. 'For once in my life I was useful. I only wish I could have stuck at it longer.'

'You couldn't?'

'I was there longer than anyone else on the team,' Hugh said seriously. 'In those conditions you get one thing wrong with you after another. In the end I had three nasty infections running into each other and I was ordered to leave.'

'So why not back to Edinburgh?'

Hugh turned and looked at her. His eyes crinkled into a lazy grin. 'Not done with questions yet?'

'I'll let you know when I'm through,' Leah said easily.

He hesitated and for a moment Leah wondered whether he would stop. When he finally started speaking the pain was back in his voice.

'I wrote from Ethiopia. When I first arrived I wrote to my parents, and, believe it or not, I wrote to Jane.' He frowned at the remembrance of a more naïve Hugh Kendall. 'I'd been engaged to Jane for six months and we'd been together for two years before that. I couldn't believe that she was as mercenary as she was behaving. I thought it was just a matter of time to let her know that I was serious.'

'It didn't work, though?' Leah asked sympathetically. Remembrance of her own recent conflict with Warwick flooded back.

Hugh nodded. 'I never heard back from her.'

'Or from your family?'

He gave a wintry smile. 'Birthdays and Christmas my mother writes. All about the successes of everyone else in the family. She never enquires about me.'

'Oh, Hugh, I'm sorry.' Leah uttered the words before she could stop herself.

'Don't be,' he said roughly. 'It's taught me some very valuable lessons about human nature. I'm a much more hardened member of the human race now.'

'You mean you don't trust anyone.'

'Why should I?' he asked bitterly. 'It's always the same. The mercenary motive is always there.'

'That's a bitter judgement.'

'True though,' he said softly.

Leah nodded. 'Like my treatment of my great-uncle.' She said it without rancour. His judgement of her was becoming almost her protection against him.

He nodded slowly. 'You are a beautiful woman, Leah Craig. If it weren't for the fact that I know you are capable of uncaring, mercenary behaviour and have a boyfriend who's on the make I might be tempted.'

'To do what?' It was out before she could stop herself. It was interesting, her reaction to his insults. It was increasingly seeming as if it was simply a shield, to prevent their involvement. She turned and looked down at him.

For a long moment he lay looking up at her. The sun glinted through the trees on to the bleached gold of his hair. His blue eyes creased to see her against the sun.

'To do this.' Reaching up, he took her face between his hands and drew her down to meet him.

There was no resistance. The warmth of the sun, the scent of the eucalypts and the soft resonance of Hugh's voice had acted as a drug, gradually luring Leah further and further into a vortex of emotion. This man beside her was all that mattered.

Her mouth met his, her lips gently parting to welcome him. Her hands went up to smooth the tousled hair, to somehow soothe the aching pain of this bitter man. Her heart welled over with love.

He drew her down to him so she was lying hard against him. Her body sank against his, moulded to his muscled chest. Their lips were locked together.

His tongue came out and ran along the smooth lines of her perfect teeth, gently exploring. That done, the tongue sank deeper, searching the moist depths of her mouth.

Leah was lost in a swirling mist of love and desire. Her body was not her own. Strange sensations were rising, burning through her body, heating her to an unbearable, unquenchable fire.

Hugh's hold on her loosened and he groaned. Involuntarily she reached and held him hard against her, willing his body not to leave hers.

With one dextrous movement he pulled her around beside him, then swung his body up and over hers. For a long moment he held himself up, savouring the beauty of the face beneath his.

He must be able to see my love, she thought hazily. It was there in her eyes, her skin, her smell, her aching need of him. Surely he could see past his bitter judgement to the love that was really there?

His hand was undoing the buttons at her throat. Involuntarily she moved to help him. Then the heavy cloth was no longer between them. He was gazing at her firmly rounded breasts; the taut ripeness of her nipples.

His finger moved to touch, softly exploring their texture, their feel. Then his mouth was taking them gently into it, first one, then the other.

Leah's body was on fire. Wave after wave of urgent want swept through her. Her breasts were lifting into him as if they had a life of their own. As his hand came to loosen the fastening of her jeans she welcomed it, almost crying with joy as his fingers searched, caressing the heart of the fire within her.

She had to get closer to him. Her fingers fumbled with the buttons of his shirt until they found an entry. His skin was firm and hard. She ran her hand through the fine hairs on his chest, down through the natural pathway leading to his navel and beyond. As her fingers found the buckle of his belt and started to probe he pulled back.

'Would you let me take you?' Hugh pushed himself away and stared down at her, his eyes deep and unfathomable.

'Yes.' It was a whisper of total sublimation to the wishes of her body.

For a long moment he was still, searching her eyes. She met his fearlessly, her eyes reflecting her aching need. Then he was on his feet, roughly adjusting his clothes.

'Get up,' he said harshly. He reached down a hand and pulled her to her feet. 'Otherwise I'm going to do something we'd both regret.'

'Are you sure we'd regret it?' she asked softly.

'We've taken no precautions. I'm not particularly fussed about landing in a situation where I'd be forced to marry you.'

Leah gasped. For a moment she stared at him speechlessly, before shaking her head.

'Fate worse than death?' she asked quietly. 'To be forced to marry one of these mercenary members of the human race?' She met his look as she fastened her clothes. Gathering her dignity about her, she gave him one last hard look and retreated to her car.

Only as she emerged from the farm's road gate did she finally allow her hurt and humiliation to show. By the time she had pulled up outside her own little farmhouse she could barely see through her tears. For a long time she couldn't move. She sat, her head bowed on the steering-wheel, and wept.

CHAPTER NINE

LEAH lay awake long into the night. The patterns of the moonlight shifted across the ceiling as the night took its course, yet still sleep would not come.

Leah's body ached with an unfulfilled desire. Her pride lay in tatters about her.

She had offered herself to Hugh Kendall as she had offered herself to no man before. He had known she had wanted him. He had taken her to the point where he knew she had no resistance and then left her.

She tossed fitfully on the hard bed. Finally, with the knowledge that sleep wasn't going to come, she rose and went out on to the veranda.

It was a still, warm night, with a full moon casting a soft light over the countryside. On a normal night the place could have soothed and settled Leah's fears. Tonight there was no peace.

She was wrong, she told herself sadly, to offer herself to him like that. Naïve, perhaps, another voice told her. But not wrong. Surely it wasn't wrong to offer love?

What if she had told him the true story of her great-uncle? she asked herself. Would it have made a difference?

She shook her head, knowing instinctively the truth of her decision. Hugh Kendall had been wounded. His trust had been destroyed, by his family and by his love. He was looking for flaws. If he didn't believe she had

wilfully ignored the old man, he would believe something else of her. His belief in the people close to him
was soured, tainted by the behaviour of too many
others.

One day, Leah said to herself firmly; one day he'll
come with doubt in his eyes and say, 'I don't believe
you are capable of doing such a thing.' One day. . .

She smiled to herself ruefully and shook her head.
She was dreaming like the child she was acting.

The clock on the mantel inside struck three and Leah
rose stiffly. There were mosquitoes out here and, if she
didn't move, by the morning she'd look like something
out of the quarantine wards. As she walked inside the
phone rang.

She grimaced. The last thing she needed was a call
back to the hospital. She picked up the phone with a
sinking heart.

'Leah?'

'Hugh.' She gazed blankly at the receiver, frozen to
the spot.

'Were you awake?'

'Yes.' It was a whisper.

'Can I come over?'

Leah was silent for a long moment. Tell him to get
lost, her head was saying. He doesn't love you or trust
you. Be sensible. Look after yourself.

It wasn't her head that answered. 'Yes,' she said
softly.

'Are you sure?'

She smiled gently. 'How about those precautions you
said we hadn't taken?'

When he replied she could hear an answering smile
in the voice at the other end. 'There have to be a few
advantages to being the town's acting pharmacist.'

'I'll see you soon, then.'

'Soon.' It was a soft echo of her words.

She sat in the window and waited. As his headlights picked their way along the track she went outside and stood at the top of the steps. His vehicle came to a halt just beneath her.

There was no doubt in her heart. Whatever the motives of Hugh Kendall, Leah knew that for her this was right. She was twenty-seven years old and for the first time in her life she loved a man. Hugh had judged her and found her wanting. She had judged him and fallen in love.

If he ever loves me and trusts me it will be a bonus, she told herself. For now, all I care about is being as close to him as I can, staying with him for as long as I can. Tomorrow can take care of itself.

There was no pride in what Leah was doing, but she knew instinctively that to hold out in pride against Hugh Kendall would be to abandon any chance of breaking down the wall of distrust he had built up around himself.

He was out of the driver's seat, looking up uncertainly at the slight figure standing above him.

Leah hadn't put on a robe. The soft white silk of her nightdress fell in gentle folds around her. It was cut low across her breasts, with two tiny ribbons of satin holding it across the smooth skin of her shoulders. Leah's hair, tousled by her vain attempts to find sleep, fell in a mass of tangled curls around her face. Her eyes stood out, dark and unreadable in her too pale face.

For a long moment they stayed there, immovable, each waiting for the other to break the silence. Leah felt as if her heart was going to burst. The look of the big man standing below her filled her with love and desire to the point where she thought she must go crazy.

Blindly she lifted a hand and reached out. Somehow the steps between them ceased to exist and she was being held, held as if this man could never let her go.

For an eternity they stood locked there, each not wanting to break the moment. For Leah it was enough that these strong hands were around her, her body being held hard against the man she loved.

It was Hugh who broke the silence. His hands slid down the silken sheen of her nightgown, feeling the rounded contours of her body. He broke away and stood back, holding her at arm's length as she gazed at him wonderingly.

'Eh, but you're lovely, lass,' he said softly.

Leah met his look and smiled. She lifted a hand and ran it lightly down his cheek, feeling the strong bone-structure of his face. She stroked her fingers along his strong jaw then brought them back again to lightly touch his lips. He reached and took her hand into his, kissing it lightly. His eyes didn't leave her face.

'I couldn't sleep,' he said quietly. 'You stayed with me.' He shook his head. 'I'm mad, I know, but in the end I couldn't help myself. I had to come.'

Leah looked up into the uncertainty of Hugh's eyes. It was as if he was acting against his better judgement, being drawn into something he had no control over. She smiled faintly. 'I'm not something to battle against,' she said gently. 'I'm not something to choose against your better judgement.'

He looked wryly down at her. 'I'm not sure I have any judgement any more.'

'You mean, if you did, you wouldn't be here?'

He was silent, his hands moving slowly through the waving softness of her hair.

'I don't know,' he said finally. His hands dropped to her waist and gripped. He closed his eyes as if in pain. 'I swore a long time ago that I would never commit myself to any long-term relationship.'

He took a deep breath.

'That's still true, Leah. I'd be a bastard if I didn't make that clear. All I know, at the moment, is that I want you, that I can't think straight for wanting you. So I'm here. If you want me to get lost, then say so. But say so quickly because——' his voice broke and dropped to being almost a whisper '—if I stand here looking at you for much longer I'm not going to be responsible for what I might do.'

Leah ran her hands lightly down the strong arms at her waist. Her heart twisted in pain for this man before her.

'You want me,' she whispered. 'That's all I care about tonight.'

'And tomorrow?'

All Leah's reservations were gone. The moonlight was shining its soft light, catching Hugh's face and reflecting the doubt and desire. Mingled with it was something else. Loneliness, she thought suddenly and knew with certain truth that she, who had lost her family as a teenager, had never been as alone as this man.

She reached for the buttons of his shirt. Unfastening them with slow deliberation, she reached in to feel the warmth of his body within.

'Tomorrow,' she said, her voice suddenly rich and firm, 'is for tomorrow.'

He looked down at the top of her head, feeling the light touch of her fingers as they explored his body.

'You're sure?' His voice was not quite steady.

She raised her face to his, mutely inviting his kiss. 'What do you think, Hugh Kendall?' she mocked softly. 'What do you think?'

Then suddenly their need was unbearable. Hugh gave a low, triumphant laugh and Leah was in his arms, being lifted and carried into the house, into the bedroom where an hour before she had lain in misery.

There was no misery now. She lay, wide-eyed, watching with awe as the man above her divested himself of his clothes.

The sight of him made her catch her breath. His superb body, muscled and lean, filled the room. Leah watched him in the moonlight, glorying in the maleness of him.

He lifted her to stand against him, reaching down to catch the flimsy nightwear and lift it over her head. Then she was lowered, back on to the bed, and his body came down to meet hers.

Flesh against flesh, skin against skin, full length they lay against each other. Leah reached up and ran her hands lightly down his body, then up to take the beloved face into her hands to find his mouth.

He kissed her searchingly, as if seeking for a deeper truth. Their hands explored, seeking knowledge that only touch could give them.

Leaving her mouth, Hugh's kisses moved elsewhere, behind her ears, down to the hollow of her throat, across the deep valley formed by her breasts and beyond. As he reached the flatness of her stomach his face came to rest, the roughness of his cheek stirring across the satin-smoothness of her skin.

His hands stroked her inner thighs, sending shards of pleasure through her. As he gently parted her thighs his face moved again, kissing her lightly, his fingers feeling for the parts which would give her pleasure.

Her body was a whirling fire, a red-hot flame with its centre under this man's probing fingers. Tears of pleasure were running down her face. Leah was no longer moving. Her hands lay limply at her sides. Her body was his.

Then the fingers stopped. He raised himself so that he was searching her face, seeking to know her in the moonlight. His fingers traced the course of a tear.

She couldn't bear it. She reached for and held his body, pulling it down to meet hers, demanding him to possess her. She arched to meet him. With a groan he sank, deep, deep into the moist depths of her innermost being.

It was right. This man in this place was right; it was as it should be. The pain, when it came, was sharp and sweet. Leah cried out, then again in swift protest as she felt him hesitate. She moved down to hold him into her.

Again she was gathered against him. Their bodies moved in perfect rhythm. Leah rose and fell against him, each time moving to a new level of awareness, a new peak of being.

When they came, they came together in a blinding crescendo that left her feeling as if nothing in this life could ever be the same.

Afterwards Hugh raised himself on one elbow and looked wonderingly down at the naked figure beside him. He touched her face lightly.

'It was your first time.' It wasn't a question.

'Yes.' Leah was sated, sleepy with love.

'What about Warwick?' The harsh question jarred in the night. Leah thought about it in silence for a moment before answering. Finally she responded simply with the truth.

'Warwick was my boyfriend, not my lover.'

'Was?'

'Was.'

He was silent for a moment and Leah could sense his puzzlement. One of this man's judgements was being proved wrong. She looked up at him, his dark form rising above her. Unable to help herself she ran her hand lightly through the short, curling hair of his chest. Reaching up she kissed him lightly, then buried her face against him.

He fell back on to the pillow, holding her loosely against him. Her hair tumbled across his chest and he ran his fingers through the tangled curls.

'Am I your lover, then?' he said lightly.

Leah pushed herself up so that she was looking directly into his eyes. The feel of him under her was sweeping away her sleepiness. She placed a finger against his lips and dropped a kiss on his forehead.

'You are my love,' she said softly. After that there was no need for words for a very long time.

The sound of Dora at the window finally woke them. She was a sheep of avid curiosity and had early in the piece discovered she could find Leah by climbing on to the veranda. Her soft bleating made the figures in the bed stir, and Leah opened her eyes.

'Go away,' she said softly to the ewe. 'You'll wake him.'

'I'm already awake.' Hugh didn't move or open his eyes. 'I hope to hell you're only talking to the sheep.'

Leah grinned. 'What if I were to tell you there was a deputation from Citizens Against Moral Decay standing at our bedroom window right now?'

'I wouldn't believe you,' he said firmly, reaching over to pull her against him. 'I would have heard their thumps as they fainted dead away by now. Come here, woman.'

Leah wiggled from his clasp and stood up. He opened his eyes.

'What are you doing?'

'What does it look like?'

He lay still, considering, as she started gathering clothes.

'It looks to me like you're getting up.'

'Very good,' she said approvingly. 'I thought I might just take a shower.'

'What an excellent idea,' Hugh approved. He rose, took her clothes firmly away from her and laid them on the bed. 'Let's both have one.'

'We won't fit.'

'Let's try,' Hugh said patiently. 'Anything's possible if we give it our best shot.'

An hour later, weak with laughter and with a bathroom awash with soapy water, Leah finally completed her shower.

'There.' Hugh carried her glowing body back into the bedroom and deposited her triumphantly on the bed. 'I told you it was possible.'

'It is not,' Leah choked. 'I've still got soap behind my ears and in all sorts of other places.'

'Let me check,' Hugh said solicitously. He reached down and ran a tongue tentatively behind her ear.

'Ugh. You're right. Now, where else did you say you still had it?'

'I didn't.' Leah shoved him backwards and pulled a sheet around herself. 'Get away from me, Hugh Kendall, or I'm going to have to take another shower and I don't think I'm strong enough. I've a suspicion I'm going to be black and blue from the last one and how am I going to explain that to Matron?' She stood up and backed away from the bed. 'Now leave me be to get dressed. I've patients who need seeing even if yours don't apparently need you.'

He sighed and reached for his trousers. 'You're right, of course, lass.' He smiled up at her, his slow, all-embracing smile that made Leah's heart lurch within her. 'It was fun while it lasted.'

Leah's smile died. 'Fun while it lasted.' Was that how he would always see it?

She caught herself. She had known the terms at the beginning and had accepted Hugh at his word. She couldn't demand anything more of him now. With a struggle she kept the lightness in her voice as she replied.

'We were lucky to have a whole night.' Then a thought struck her. 'Or did we?' She frowned. 'What if the hospital was trying to locate you?'

Hugh motioned down to his belt. Strapped to it was the receiver for his radio.

'We would have heard about it.'

'How convenient,' Leah smiled. 'For use when visiting young ladies.'

'Or pregnant ewes,' Hugh agreed sagely. 'Mostly until now it's been pregnant ewes.' He reached over and touched Leah lightly on the nose. 'My ratio of young ladies versus pregnant ewes has been pretty dismal. I think, from here on in, I intend to work on it.'

Leah smiled, though it cost her an effort. Keep it light, she told herself. It was the only way.

'You do that,' she told him.

CHAPTER TEN

IT HAD been a quiet night at the hospital. Leah's ward round was done with speed. There was still not a huge number of patients officially hers. The patients who had long-term, complex illnesses were, in the main, being treated by Hugh, the doctor they had been seeing for the longer time. Leah had enough to keep her busy for an hour and a half. If there was no accident or emergency it promised to be a quiet day.

Mrs Robinson was sitting up in bed, nursing her little girl. She beamed up at Leah as she entered.

'Oh, Dr Craig, isn't she the most gorgeous thing? Look, she can suck. She knows just what to do.' She twisted so that Leah could clearly see how talented her newborn baby was. 'Mum says when I was born I wouldn't suck for ages.' She beamed mistily down at the fuzzy head at her breast. 'She's going to be much cleverer than I am, Dr Craig. I can tell.'

Leah smiled. Perching on the edge of the bed, she touched the soft little head. 'Maybe,' she said non-committally. 'I think you're pretty clever to produce this perfect little specimen.'

The girl flushed with pleasure and held the baby tighter. She looked up, suddenly shy.

'Thank you for not making me have a Caesarian,' she said seriously. 'Mum had me by Caesarian and she always reckoned it spoiled it a bit.'

'In your mother's day they would have had to put

135

her completely to sleep,' Leah said. 'And a general anaesthetic generally makes you feel pretty lousy.'

'She was pretty sore afterwards, she said.'

'And you're not?' Leah grinned. 'After a full forceps delivery you deserve to be sore.'

'Yeah, OK.' The woman smiled agreement. 'Perhaps I just haven't come down from the clouds to feel it yet.' She bit her lip and hesitated. 'I know I shouldn't question it, and Doug, my husband, says I nearly had to have a Caesarian so I should be grateful, but did I really need the forceps?'

Leah nodded. This was to be expected. After nine months of intensive education on natural childbirth it was starting to be common for new mothers to feel as if they had personally failed if there had to be intervention.

'*You* didn't need it,' she said gently. She stretched out and lightly touched a tiny cheek. 'This little one did. After thirty-six hours in transit she was just plain exhausted.' She smiled. 'If we'd let her come in her own good time she might still have made it, but she was starting to show signs of distress. Her pulse rate was dropping and we were seeing meconium-stained liquor. That showed she was in trouble. And frankly,' she looked up at the questioning mother, 'she was just too precious to take the risk.'

Mrs Robinson looked down at the tiny bundle at her breast. She looked up again at Leah and her eyes were glistening with tears. 'Thank you,' she said simply.

'It was Dr Kendall who did most of the work,' Leah said fairly.

She nodded. 'I know you called him in and I'm grateful. It's you who were with me for the labour though. I'd like to stay as your patient, if that's all right with you.' She looked down again at the baby. 'Emma Louise and I. And Doug too probably, although he's not too sure how he'll go with a lady doctor. After last night he said he'd give it a go, though. That is,' she looked questioningly at Leah, 'if you've decided to stay at Carslake long term. Dr Kendall said at the beginning that you might only be temporary.'

'I don't know,' Leah said. 'At the moment I'm afraid I still don't know.' She picked up the now replete baby and placed her carefully back in her crib. 'Just for a moment,' she apologised to the sleeping infant. 'Your mum can spend the rest of the day cuddling you, but just for a moment I need to check her tummy.'

Mrs Robinson was her last patient. Hugh had gone back to the farm to check his precious sheep before coming in to do his ward round. As Leah emerged from the hospital entrance his disreputable vehicle pulled up.

'A bit tardy today, aren't we, Doctor?' she asked primly, glancing pointedly at her watch.

Hugh laughed and deviated from his course to touch her lightly as they passed. 'If nothing crops up here I'll be over this afternoon,' he promised.

Leah raised her eyebrows non-committally. 'I'll check my diary and see if I'm otherwise engaged.'

His smile broadened. 'You do that, Dr Craig. Open your diary to this afternoon and write in big letters, "Spraying blackberries with Dr Kendall".'

Leah sighed. 'I should have known you were offering something no girl could resist.'

She drove home with happiness circling her, enveloping her with warmth and light. So what if he didn't love her? she told herself confidently. He would. One day he would.

* * *

The blackberry-spraying was destined to be postponed. Leah hadn't been home for half an hour before she was disturbed by the phone.

'There's been a car smash over at Blythe's Ridge,' the duty sister said apologetically. 'We've only just received the call and we're not sure on details, but it seems a car full of teenagers has gone over the edge. That's about all we know. It could be nothing but it could be nasty.' The girl hesitated and then went on. 'Knowing Blythe's Ridge, I'd say it would probably be the latter. Dr Kendall has gone out with the ambulance. He asked if you could make preparations here for the possibility of multiple casualties.'

Leah's heart sank. In her time in Casualty these were the accidents she dreaded most: kids in cars.

'I'll be right in,' she said.

By the end of the day whatever joy Leah had been feeling had evaporated as if it had never been.

There had been six kids in the car. According to a shaken driver who had been travelling behind they had come around the bluff at the end of the ridge without slowing down. The drop was unforgiving. Two of them were dead. The other four were so badly injured that, if they did survive, which in a couple of cases was doubtful, they would carry the scars for the rest of their lives.

Every available nurse was called back to the hospital. Leah and Hugh worked frantically, trying desperately to save the lives that the teenagers themselves had deemed so unimportant.

The first youth had died instantly. The second died under Leah's hands on the operating table as they fought desperately to relieve pressure from a massive head wound.

Because of the enormity of the accident the air ambulance came supplied with a fully equipped medical team. Two hours after the accident Hugh and Leah were joined by two other doctors. There was little left for them to do, other than to supervise the transport of the injured kids to the waiting aircraft. Their injuries were too complex to be dealt with at Carslake.

As they walked back into the hospital Leah found that she was shaking. She glanced across at Hugh to find him watching her with concern.

'Do you want me to do this?' he asked quietly. There were still the families to be faced, the families of the two youngsters who had died.

Leah shook her head. 'No,' she said, taking a deep breath. 'Two deaths, two families, two doctors.' She hesitated for a moment at the entrance, waiting until she was sure she had herself under control. Then, with a tiny nod at Hugh, she went ahead.

Afterwards she went back outside. Hugh was still with the family of the boy who had died first.

Leah watched the car of the parents she had just talked to as it disappeared up the road. From lunchtime to now—she glanced at the watch—four short hours and their life had been irrevocably changed. To lose a child. . .

She thought back to Mrs Robinson, bursting with love and pride on the arrival of her little girl. There was no guarantee that eighteen years from now she wouldn't suffer the same anguish.

Leah left the steps and made her way to the bushland behind the hospital. Inside the building everyone was still busy, as nursing staff cleaned up and caught up on the tasks that had been abandoned for the afternoon. Leah couldn't face them.

Her mind went back to the afternoon fourteen years ago when a policeman had come to fetch her from school and tell her that her parents had been killed.

Her hands clenched. It all seemed so futile. And transient, she thought bitterly. Maybe that was why she was so ready to give herself to Hugh Kendall, a man who didn't really love or trust her. It didn't last.

He found her there, half an hour later. She was seated on a fallen log, just out of sight of the hospital building. The worst of the pain had passed; now she was left with an overwhelming sense of desolation and hopelessness.

Hugh came along the path and stopped as he saw her. She didn't move.

'Leah?'

She didn't answer. He stooped to take her cold hands in his.

'Leah, what is this? You must have coped with accidents before.'

She laughed mirthlessly. 'Maybe that was why I wanted to be a radiologist.'

He looked at her for a long moment. 'You mean you don't like getting involved?'

'Who does?' she asked bitterly. 'Certainly not the self-contained Hugh Kendall.'

He was silent. Leah looked up to find his expression grim and distant.

'I'm sorry,' she said quietly. Hugh had worked as hard as anyone could—harder—to save the lives of the teenagers, and Leah had caught his expression over the operating table as they had lost the child they were working on. Professional detachment was a long way away. Detachment from her though. . . That was a different thing.

She stood stiffly.

'I'm sorry you had to come looking for me. Did you need me?'

'No.' The grim look was still there.

'I'll be getting back, then.' She made to turn away but Hugh's grip on her hands was still strong. He was looking at her, a crease running between his eyes.

'You did care back there.' There was puzzlement, as if he was trying to come to terms with something.

Leah pulled her hands away. 'Contrary to what you believe, Hugh Kendall, I am still capable of involvement.' Her voice broke. 'I just wish to hell I wasn't.'

She left him standing, staring after her as she retreated back to the hospital, away from the bitter judgements of Hugh Kendall.

It was early evening when she arrived back at the farm. Tomorrow was Monday and she hadn't done half the things she had intended for the weekend, but they would have to wait. She was caught in a sea of confusion. Happy or unhappy?

This morning she had thought she only had to be near Hugh Kendall to be at peace, calmly accepting him as her man. Tonight?

To live for the moment. It had been her philosophy since her parents had died, to live one day at a time and not question the future.

Why had the deaths of two kids made her question it? Surely it should have backed her up, consolidated her belief in the now rather than the future?

She was changing though. She acknowledged it to herself with sudden clarity. The Leah Craig whom Hugh Kendall had attacked on the farm steps two months ago was not the Leah Craig of now. It was as though an outer layer of skin were being peeled off, leaving a softer, more vulnerable surface exposed to the elements.

Leah mechanically made herself some tea and went out on the veranda to eat. The sun was setting in a crimson haze on the horizon. Below the veranda, Dora and Henry watched her every move.

She was going to have to do something about this farm. Her brain veered from the emotional turmoil it had been caught in, and engaged itself in practicalities. Dora and Henry weren't enough to keep the bush at bay. If she was going to keep this farm she was going to have to do it properly.

But how? She didn't know the first thing about farming and, if she continued to work at her present rate at Carslake, she wasn't going to have time to learn. And did she want to stay at Carslake?

She had drifted into this job, she acknowledged, and for the first time she made herself see why. It was double-edged, she knew. She had wanted to put down roots and belong to this place, and she had wanted to be near Hugh Kendall.

And now?

She left the veranda and made her way down the rough track to the river. Dora and Henry nosed along behind her, delighted that their human was doing something interesting.

They stopped as she reached the sandy cove where she had rescued the lamb. Sheep had a reputation for stupidity but for these two the memory of their recent trauma seemed to be still vivid.

'You can't fall in here, you silly things,' Leah told them. 'It's only when you've got a cliff you need to worry.'

They didn't believe her. They stopped as the bush

turned into sand and stood watching her, a concerned expression on Dora's woolly face.

It's as if she's worried about me, Leah thought wryly and smiled. It was nice to know someone worried about her, even if it was only a sheep.

Despite the ewe's concern the water was calling. Leah hadn't been in the river since she had rescued Henry, and hesitated for a moment, but the need was too great. She slipped off her clothes and slid into the cool water.

It was balm to her confused mind and tired body. She floated on her back, watching the last of the light, softly pink above the trees. In the canopy of leaves a host of tiny birds flitted back and forth, rushing to bring the last of the day's provisions back to their nests before darkness enveloped them. The soft rustle they made in the leaves and the distant squawking of a flock of cockatoos were the only sounds that broke the stillness.

It was too hard, Leah thought drearily. To drift was becoming impossible, and yet to make decisions about the future was impossible too.

The practical course was to put this place on the market and find a job somewhere where she could learn to be independent, away from Hugh Kendall.

Away from Hugh Kendall. Away from his criticisms, his judgements. Away from his smile and his touch.

It was too hard.

There was another death that night, the expected death of an old man in the nursing-home section of the hospital. Leah went in to the hospital when the call came. An hour later, as her watch announced the beginning of a new day and she could at last head home to bed, she passed Hugh's vehicle on the road. She flinched for him. Hopefully at last she could now get some sleep. Hugh must have just been called out.

Despite the emotional turmoil of the day she slept the sleep of the exhausted. She woke feeling as if at least she could cope with the day ahead.

One day at a time, she told herself bitterly as she again turned out of her driveway. That's all you're capable of.

The day was long and hard. The town was in shock. In such a tiny community the death and injury of six teenagers left no one unaffected. Leah saw one shocked relative after another and, in the adjoining clinic, knew that Hugh was doing the same. The parents of the injured were in Melbourne with their children, but there were still aunts and uncles, siblings, grandparents and friends.

Leah admitted one old lady suffering from chest pain. She was the grandmother of one of the injured girls. Her daughter, the girl's aunt, brought the old lady in.

'It's not fair,' the aunt said bitterly as Leah and she came out of the old lady's room. 'They just don't think. They put their lives at risk and don't think of the others they're risking in the process.' She gestured backwards to the closed door.

'Mum thinks the world of Karen. Karen's parents have got a dairy farm and all the time Karen was a baby she used to stay with Mum during the milking, night and morning. Now Mum's got a heart condition and is just about house-bound, her whole life revolves around the family. I'll bet Karen didn't give that a thought when she was hurtling round the hills with her friends.'

'The young don't,' Leah said softly. She thought back to her own parents, killed in a high-speed crash. 'And sometimes the not so young. At least Karen might have the chance to learn from her mistakes and start again.' The bulletin from the city hospital that morning had been encouraging.

The girl's aunt nodded. She looked as if she had not slept the night before, and her eyes were swollen with weeping. 'I'm sorry. I know we should be grateful that at least she's alive. My neighbour's kid isn't though.' She shook her head. 'That ridge is the most dangerous piece of road in the district and they didn't even slow down.' Her voice shook. 'If they weren't dead or dreadfully injured I'd put a belt to the lot of them.'

Leah smiled ruefully. 'I think those that survive will have learned a dreadful lesson.'

The woman looked up at her wonderingly. 'How do you cope?' she asked suddenly. 'It's hard enough for us who have to cope once in our lives, but for you to have to deal with this sort of thing every day. . .'

'Hardly every day,' Leah said quietly. 'Though when I worked in city casualty I did see a lot of it.' She bit her lip. 'You never get used to it. I cried last night too.'

'Honestly?'

'Honestly.'

The woman gazed up into Leah's face and believed her. 'Are you staying here permanently?' she asked abruptly.

'I don't know.'

They had walked to where the corridor led back to Leah's rooms. A queue of patients waited for her. As she turned to leave the woman placed a restraining hand on Leah's arm.

'I hope you do,' she said sincerely. 'We'd be the poorer without you.'

Then she was gone. Leah watched her go, then took a deep breath and went to deal with the next patient.

By the time Leah had coped with her morning surgery it was nearly three in the afternoon. Lunch was long past. There had been five admissions though, and her afternoon work was banking up. For a moment Leah contemplated not having a break at all and then rejected the idea. The way she was going, another fifteen minutes or so would hardly matter. It was going to be nine at night before she finished anyway. She gave her last card back to Rosie and went to find Mrs Ross.

That lady looked up as Leah entered the kitchen and eyed her appraisingly.

'I was wondering where you'd got to.'

'Do you think I could borrow a couple of slices of bread for a sandwich?' Leah asked apologetically. 'I missed lunch.'

'I noticed,' Mrs Ross said dourly. 'Sit yourself down.'

'I can get it myself,' Leah protested. She gestured towards the pastry the cook had been kneading. 'You're busy.'

'No need.' Mrs Ross reached into the refrigerator and bought out a plate laden with cold chicken and salad. A crusty roll with delicate curls of butter beside it on the plate, fragrant coffee from the pot bubbling on the stove and Leah's lunch was complete. 'If you hadn't arrived in the next ten minutes I was going to come and find you,' she explained.

'Thank you,' Leah said simply and applied herself to the food.

For a while there was silence in the kitchen, save for the odd clink of Leah's cutlery and the gentle pounding of pastry against the table. Mrs Ross let Leah finish her meal and begin her coffee before breaking her self-imposed quiet.

'Now, would you like to talk about it?'

'Talk about what?'

Mrs Ross looked at her consideringly. 'Whatever it is that's bothering you.'

Leah put her cup down carefully on the saucer. This lady was too darn all-seeing.

'I guess I'm upset about the kids,' she admitted. 'It was such a waste.'

Mrs Ross nodded. 'Aren't we all? I'm thinking though that the strain you're showing behind your eyes can't be totally explained by something you must have met before and will meet again. Their deaths will have upset you but they won't have made you look as if you've got a problem too big for you to face.'

Leah wrinkled her nose. 'Mrs Ross, I'm not exactly sure I like having my face analysed.'

'Then don't come into my kitchen,' the lady said unrepentantly.

Leah sighed and reached for the coffee-pot to refill her cup. 'If you didn't make such lovely coffee, I wouldn't.' She glanced at her watch and grimaced. 'I shouldn't be doing this.'

Mrs Ross stopped her pounding and surveyed the slight figure in front of her. Leah might be a doctor but she was young enough to be her daughter. Mrs Ross had brought up three girls and had always been able to sense when something was really wrong. This slip of a girl was giving her the same message.

'You're in love with him, aren't you?' It was a guess,

but even as she said it she was confident she was right. Leah's eyes flew up to meet hers, dismay etched on her face.

'I. . . How did you know?'

'There,' Mrs Ross said in satisfaction. 'Can't I always tell?' She went back to her rhythmic pounding, her attention seemingly solely devoted to her pastry. 'And him?' she asked, seemingly of the pastry beneath her hands. She paused and stared reflectively out of the window across the hospital courtyard. Finally she answered her own question. 'I guess not, or you wouldn't be looking so darn unhappy.' She pursed her lips. 'Have you told him the truth about your great-uncle yet?'

Leah shook her head. 'No. And I don't intend to. It wouldn't make any difference.'

'It did with me.'

Again Leah shook her head. 'Mrs Ross, I didn't have to tell you that story. You judged me and knew that the story didn't fit. I didn't have to talk you out of believing I was a money-grubbing, uncaring human being. You felt there had to be some explanation.'

'And with Dr Kendall?'

'He believes the worst,' Leah said bitterly. 'Everything good about me catches him by surprise. It's no use feeding him any more good bits because, deep down, he doesn't trust and he can't love.' She stared down sightlessly into the dregs of her coffee-mug.

'But you do trust and you do love?' Mrs Ross said gently.

'Yes.' Leah rose and carried her cup to the sink, then turned to meet Mrs Ross's concerned gaze. 'I just don't know whether I've got enough love and trust for the both of us.'

CHAPTER ELEVEN

LEAH hardly saw Hugh all that day. There seemed to be a huge amount of work for them both and the telephone didn't stop. Every time there was a moment to catch their breath they were answering frantic questions from relatives. What did the hospital bulletins mean? What were the chances of survival? What would the long term hold for these injured teenagers?

By the time she had finished it was nearly midnight. How on earth had Hugh coped on his own? Leah asked herself as she made a hot drink before going to bed. Yesterday's accident had been a one-off tragedy that, hopefully, wouldn't occur again for years, and yet it had showed glaringly that this community had to have two doctors.

What would happen when she left? The thought came into her head and she let it lie, quietly considering it.

What she was doing at the moment was almost worse than not being here at all. She was beginning to build up her practice of patients who were expecting to see her. The community was starting to realise that its members could see a doctor when they wanted to, rather than wait for weeks or go to the city. When she left. . . The question hung.

It all depended, she told herself. On what? She had gone into this job thinking it would depend on her suitability for general practice. Now she was seeing very clearly that general practice was what she wanted to do. She wanted this job, this community. . .and Hugh Kendall.

As if her thoughts had summoned him, the lights of his vehicle appeared at the end of her track. Leah put down her cup and went outside to meet him. She stood calmly on the veranda, waiting for him to come to her.

'I wasn't going to come,' he said quietly, coming up the steps to her. He stopped a little way from her. 'I saw your light still on from the road.'

'I've only just come home,' she said.

He nodded. 'I thought you must have. It's been one hell of a day.' He looked at her directly. 'Thank you. I wouldn't have coped without you.'

'You have before.'

'Not with something as major as this.' He paused reflectively. 'Or perhaps I have and not realised what having adequate help can mean. Without you the urgent medicine would have been performed. There would have been no comfort for those most in need of it though. To be able to stop and explain things to relatives has been one of the biggest bonuses of your being here.'

'Long may it last.' Leah's voice contained a thread of bitterness. He glanced at her sharply.

'Are you thinking of leaving?'

'Not yet.'

'When?'

She couldn't help herself. 'When you stop wanting me,' she said simply.

There was silence.

'You're good,' he said at last. 'If you'd like to stay at Carslake permanently you know the position is yours.'

'That's not what I meant.' She paused and then went on. 'Hugh, I can't stay here loving you.'

'Loving me?' The words echoed oddly around them.

'That's what I said.'

Hugh closed his eyes. Fatigue was etched on his face.
'I'm sorry,' he said shortly. 'I shouldn't have come.'

Pain welled in Leah's heart. This man was fighting
against himself.

'Why not?'

He looked at her in the faint light from the open
door and shook his head.

'Why did you come?' she insisted.

'Because I wanted you.' The words were forced out.

She took three steps until she came to him, not
stopping until her breasts were against his chest. She
reached around and held him gently to her.

'Why do you want me?' she asked gently. 'Because
you want a woman? Or something more?'

He looked down at her helplessly.

'Do you just want me?' she asked inexorably. 'Or do
you love me, Hugh Kendall?'

She felt his body stiffen. His hands reached out and
pushed her away, holding her at arm's length.

'I don't love you, Leah.' He laughed bitterly. 'I don't
love anyone. Can't you understand that?'

She shook her head. 'No. I can't. You can't lose
your ability to love.' She smiled mirthlessly. 'Look at
me. I've been offended, insulted, and told that I'm
only wanted, not loved, and yet all I can do is stand
here and think how much I love you.'

She shook her head before continuing.

'That's why I'm going to have to leave. If there was
any control, any way I could say I don't love, that's
what I'd be doing. Instead of which here I am, half
silly with joy for seeing you.'

'Until tomorrow,' Hugh jeered. 'Or the next day.

Until it isn't convenient to keep loving. Then it'll be a fine excuse to leave Carslake.'

She looked up at him wonderingly. Even in the dim light Hugh could see his own pain reflected in her eyes.

'Perhaps you're right,' she said softly. 'Perhaps it's like that. You've loved people before and you've learned to judge. Perhaps after I've loved you for a while I'll be as bitter.'

'Leah. . .'

She was silent.

'I'll go,' he finally said.

Still she was silent, her face still and expressionless.

'Leah. . .' It was all there, in the single word, the pain, the confusion and the longing. For a moment he gazed down at Leah's pale face and the last vestige of his control broke. She was pulled fiercely into his arms.

The gentleness of the night before had gone. Hugh's need was a fierce, overwhelming hunger, driving him to possess her. His mouth was locked against hers, his hands already searching to loosen the soft fabric of her dress.

For a moment Leah resisted, holding herself rigid against him. Then, as his hand found an entry to cup a breast, she knew her body would betray her. Her nipple was taut against his fingers. Lower, a fire was alight between her thighs, burning with an ache that only this man could assuage.

She dug her fingers into his back, pulling him harder against her. The last of the buttons of her dress were unfastened. He pulled back to let the fabric fall into a crumpled heap at her feet.

Then, somehow they were in the house. There was no time, no need to find the bedroom. The rough old rug before the fire was suffice to bed them as they found the only thing that mattered; the core of each other's bodies that allowed them to become one.

They woke in the harsh light of dawn, responding to the cold and the hardness of the floor. Leah was still curled into the protective warmth of Hugh's body, her back curved to mould against the line of his chest. His hands held her, even in sleep. As she stirred he woke as well.

'I thought your bed was bad but this is ridiculous,' he muttered into her ear. From somewhere underneath her he disengaged his wrist and looked at the time. 'Damn.'

'What's wrong?'

His hands moved against the soft skin of her stomach, gently stroking. 'I have to get around the sheep. It's been twenty-four hours since I've checked them.' The soft stroking continued.

'Hugh?'

'Mmm.' He nuzzled her ear.

She pushed herself up and over so she was kneeling at his side. The sight of his nakedness in the dawn light made her gasp. He smiled at the wonder in her eyes.

'What's the matter, Dr Craig? Never seen a naked man before?'

She smiled. 'Never one that I love as much as this one,' she said quietly.

He met her eyes. For a long moment there was silence in the room. Then he sighed, a long-drawn-out sigh that seemed full of longing and regret. He reached out and pulled her up to him, up to lie full length over his body.

She was ready for him, moist and aching. As he pulled her down she took him into her body, as easily and as naturally as if they had been moulded for each other. As she felt him enter her her mind reached a pinnacle of pure joy. She moved with him on a surge of brilliant light, where her body floated in a dimension she had never dreamed of.

'There's still the sheep.'

'So there are.' Leah's voice sounded as if it were coming from a long way away. Her body was sated with love. 'Should I get up and check Dora?'

He smiled. 'I could manage to check Dora and Henry on the way out.' Somehow he found the impetus to tear himself away from the entwining warmth of their bodies. Leah stirred in protest and he lifted her as he rose.

'Barring hospital calls, my lovely Leah, you can have another two hours' sleep.' He held her against him in his arms and lightly kissed her forehead. 'I suggest you'd be a lot more comfortable in bed though.'

He tucked her between the sheets. As he bent to kiss her again her arms went out to entwine him. She found his mouth and kissed him back, a long kiss of commitment and love, given in her half-sleep. As her hands released him she was asleep again, drifting into a haze of blissful slumber.

For a long moment Hugh stayed looking down at the sleeping girl below him. Then his mouth twisted into a wry, half-mocking smile and he was gone, out to the other room to find his clothes and begin his day.

Two hours later he was back. Leah's alarm had roused her. Showered and dressed, she was halfway through her coffee and considering toast. The sound of Hugh's vehicle on the track made up her mind. She reached for the toasting fork and attached a slice of bread. By the time Hugh strode up the veranda steps she had done one slice and was starting on another.

'That's what I like.' Hugh smiled as he came in the door. 'A woman with forethought.' He reached for the butter and started spreading. 'Is that coffee brewing, or am I asleep and dreaming?'

'That's what you should be,' Leah agreed. 'Asleep and dreaming.'

He shook his head and laughed. 'Sleep? Who needs it? Sleep's only for those who are bored with being awake.'

'And you're not?'

He shook his head. 'I've just been round the flock and I have two new lambs. The sun is shining. The grass is wet with dew. The birds are making their early-morning racket and I am ready for anything.'

'For twelve hours of medicine?'

He grimaced and bit into his toast. 'Put like that, Dr Craig, perhaps sleep does have something going for it.'

Leah laughed. She poured coffee and brought the last of the toast over to the table. A warm contentment was spreading through her.

'Leah, would you like to move in with me?'

The abrupt question caught Leah by surprise and she looked up, her face a question. Hugh smiled ruefully and reached out to put a finger on her nose.

'We can't keep going on like this, you know. I had thought anything was better than that extraordinary bed of yours. After last night I've changed my mind, but only marginally. Why on earth are you putting up with lumpy kapok?'

'It's good for the soul,' Leah said defensively. 'Like cold showers and marathon running. Besides, in case you hadn't noticed, there's a dearth of furniture stores in Carslake.'

He didn't smile. His expression was suddenly serious and he turned his attention to his coffee-mug.

'Leah, you say you love me.'

'Yes,' she said simply.

He glanced up and then down again. Fingering his coffee-cup he spoke slowly.

'You know I'm not ready for the same type of commitment.' Finally he raised his head and met her eyes. 'All I know is that, for the moment, I want to be with you. I want to wake up beside you. If that's enough for you, I'd like you to stay with me.' His serious expression lightened. 'I have a proper double bed and an as new, inner-spring mattress with no lumps.'

'Wow!' Leah said lightly. 'What an incentive!'

He smiled, his smile a caress in itself. Leah returned the smile but there was doubt in her eyes.

'What's wrong?' Hugh asked gently.

'You're asking me to live with you?' she asked.

'Yes.'

'For how long?'

Hugh met her eyes. 'I don't know,' he admitted.

'Until you get me out of your system?'

Silence.

Leah sighed. Wearily she stood up and started clearing the dishes to the sink. 'What happens then?' she asked.

'I guess we go our separate ways,' he said lightly. He stood up and moved to help her with the dishes. 'Leah, I can't promise something that isn't true. I can't promise a lifetime's commitment when I don't think I'm capable of it.'

'You mean you want me now, but you're sure that something will happen in the future to sour that want?' Leah said softly.

'Yes.' The words were blunt and unequivocable.

Leah's eyes filled with tears. She turned to the man beside her.

'Is it so hard to trust?' she asked quietly. Then, at the look on his face, she turned back to the sink. Tears continued to slide down her face. 'Hugh, I don't know,' she managed to say. She was running water on to the dishes and concentrating fiercely on getting each cup meticulously clean. 'I don't know that it would work. You see, as you get me nicely out of your system I'd be getting more and more deeply involved with you.'

She glanced up at him and wasn't surprised to see the look of scepticism on his face.

'You don't think it's possible!' she burst out. Ignoring the dishes and her soapy hands, she turned to him in anger. 'You think that because you've been hurt and you're bitter then the whole world is twisted and devious. Love isn't possible in Hugh Kendall's world. And all the things I'm saying to you are meaningless.'

She put up a soapy hand and angrily brushed away a tear.

'I've put myself on the line for you, Hugh Kendall. I've thrown away any pride I used to have and told you how much I love you. It's not enough though, is it? You'd like to belittle me even more, ask me to declare myself not only to you but to all of Carslake. And for what? So that you can get me out of your system.'

'Leah——'

'And what then, Dr Kendall?' Leah was past considering what she was saying. 'What of me when you've finished with me? Can I meekly come back to this farm and keep on practising at Carslake?' She shook her head. 'You know damn well that would be impossible. I'd have lost any reputation I may have had among the local community. I'd have to leave here for good then, or have the entire community either judging me or feeling sorry for me. You wouldn't care though, would you, Dr Kendall? Would you?' Her voice broke on a sob and she turned away.

'I'm sorry,' Hugh said at last. 'I shouldn't have asked.'

'No,' Leah agreed in a muffled voice. 'You shouldn't have.' She added quietly, 'Because all my being wants to say yes, and be with you always. But I have to listen to my head. And it's starting to tell me that I'm mad, and I was mad to ever let you come near me.'

'Leah. . .'

'You'd better go,' she said quietly. 'Now, please.'

There was a long moment of silence, then Hugh turned and left. Leah stayed motionless until the last sound of his vehicle had disappeared.

She stared down into the soapy water, seeing her future bleakly before her. What had she done?

Dully she finished her task and readied herself for work. Today there was a clinic full of patients and the afternoon in theatre. Tomorrow? She winced as pain flooded through her. She had never felt so completely alone.

CHAPTER TWELVE

FOR the following few days Hugh and Leah avoided each other. They worked together, as always managing to put aside their personal friction to deal with the tasks at hand, but for the rest their communication was formal and brief.

Leah worked in a tight vacuum of pain. She was operating mechanically, trying to come to terms with an impossibility. If she was to stay at Carslake then Hugh Kendall was going to have to become a colleague, nothing more.

She found herself drifting more and more into Mrs Ross's kitchen. Without asking, that lady seemed to sense the conflict Leah was going through. Her easy chatter and comfortable silence was a soothing balm, easing the dreadful aloneness.

On the Monday after Leah had finally told Hugh to leave Mrs Ross greeted her with some news.

'Guess what?' she asked cheerily as Leah came in after her morning ward round. She took in the dark shadows under Leah's eyes and chose to ignore them. 'Wilf and Edith are home. They arrived back at the farm on Friday.'

'Oh, that's lovely.' Leah smiled. It would be good to see the elderly couple back where they belonged before she left for good.

She was going to have to leave. Every time she saw Hugh over the other side of the operating table, or striding down a corridor, Leah acknowledged to herself that she could not stay close to him for much longer without breaking down completely. She could reason with herself forever, but as soon as he entered the same room as Leah her reason collapsed into a mass of tangled emotion.

'What about going over to visit them at the weekend?' Mrs Ross was saying. Her eyes were still watching Leah, a hint of concern at the back of them.

'I. . .' Leah caught her wandering attention and smiled at Mrs Ross. 'Yes. That would be lovely.' She thought back to the last time she had seen Wilf. 'He's still going to need some medical supervision, I expect. I'll give him a ring and tell him I'm coming. It'll save him coming here.'

She left the kitchen reluctantly. As she emerged she saw Hugh coming towards her. He was holding a couple of letters in his hand and his face spelt concern. He stopped her as she passed.

'Leah, this is a report on Wilf Harvey from City Central. He's back home.'

'I know,' Leah said quietly. She looked up at him. 'Has something gone wrong? You look worried.'

He shook his head. 'Not with Wilf.' He gestured to the other letter in his hand. 'This is from Scotland. It seems my father had a stroke a week or so ago.'

Leah frowned. 'A week ago?'

'More,' he said abruptly. He referred to the letter again. 'A week ago last Thursday.'

Leah grimaced, then said quietly, 'Surely it must have been minor, though, or your family would have phoned or sent a telegram.'

Hugh laughed without humour. 'You don't know my family,' he said grimly. 'I'm lucky to even have this.' He looked down at the letter in his hand. His big hand curled around the edges of the paper and he crushed it into a ball. 'From what my mother's said it sounds serious.' He closed his eyes. 'Ten days ago! Anything could have happened.'

'Well, you phone, then,' Leah said calmly. She glanced at her watch. 'They'll be just about to go to bed in Scotland at the moment. It's a good time to catch them.'

Hugh opened his eyes and threw the letter savagely into the waste-paper basket. He looked at Leah but she knew he wasn't seeing her.

'I will,' he said shortly. He handed Leah the hospital report on Wilf. 'Here you are. He's your patient.'

'He may want to come back to you,' Leah protested.

Hugh gave a faint smile. 'If ever you deserved a patient you deserve Wilf Harvey,' he said quietly. 'If he protests I swear pigs will fly.'

They separated, Hugh to make his phone call and Leah to catch up on her correspondence before morning surgery.

Hugh's bitterness stayed with Leah as she worked. How could such a man be a product of a family like his? Or was it his imagination? She found herself hoping that he had read too much into the letter and that his father was recovering.

His smile at the end of their conversation stayed with her too. She bit her lip and the pen moving in her hand ground to a halt. The pain in her heart rose up and threatened to choke her. She loved him so much.

She bent her head again to the work at hand. Work. It was her salvation, the one constant in her life.

What could she do if she left Carslake? She knew enough about herself now to realise that she was meant to be a general practitioner. If Hugh had failed to find a doctor in the six months he had looked then there must be other remote places that needed doctors.

But did she want to go to a remote area? Perhaps it would be better if she went back to the city, where she could stay uninvolved with her patients and the community. Involvement hurt, she had discovered. Perhaps it was better to stay detached and alone.

She was getting no work done whatsoever, and almost welcomed the knock on the door when it came. Any interruption was better than this heart-wrenching decision-making.

It was Hugh. At the look on his face as he entered Leah knew that he hadn't been mistaken. For a long moment he stayed at the open door without speaking, fighting to come to terms with what he had just heard. Leah waited quietly.

'He's dying,' he said at last, fighting to get the words out. He lifted a fist and slammed it on to Leah's desk, making her pens jump. A couple fell from their holder and rolled off on to the floor. Leah ignored them.

'You talked to your mother?' she asked gently.

He laughed bitterly. 'No. I tried home and there wasn't a response. I thought she must be at the hospital so I rang there. She's gone down to London for a conference. Finally I had to speak to the ward sister to try to get any information.'

'And?'

Hugh sighed. 'He suffered a massive stroke ten days ago. Since then he's suffered a series of more minor ones which are just slowly killing him.'

Leah's eyes widened. 'Is anyone with him? Your brothers——'

'No one.' Hugh shook his head as if in pain. His hands clenched into fists on the desk in front of Leah.

Finally he fought for control. His voice, when he spoke, was tight with anger and worry.

'Leah, I'm going to have to go. I can't bear to think of him like that.' He paused and then continued. 'For the last few years we've had little to do with each other but he is my father. If the others were there. . .' His voice tailed off. 'But they're not. And I have to go.' He looked down to where she was still seated. 'Can you cope on your own?'

She nodded. 'Of course,' she said simply. Then a thought struck her. 'But not with the sheep too, Hugh.' Her voice assumed a note of panic, and despite himself Hugh smiled.

There's a farmer further up the road who's helped out before,' he reassured her. 'You'll have enough to do here to keep your hands full.' He looked at her assessingly for a moment. 'You'll be OK. The people here are considerate. You'll find they'll put off their non-urgent ailments until either I come back or they can get to the city.'

'When will you go?'

'Now. I've just rung Qantas and there's a flight I can get on this afternoon. I'm going to have to move, though.'

Leah stood up and nodded. 'So much for my correspondence.'

'It'll wait,' Hugh said with a smile back in his voice. 'It always waits, steadily growing as it does. What you have to do is separate the urgent from the non-urgent.' He picked up the pile waiting for Leah's attention. Leafing through he pulled out half a dozen letters with legal letterheads. 'These are all non-urgent,' he said firmly. 'Any letter from a lawyer is, by definition, non-urgent.'

Leah returned his smile. 'Hugh?'

He had put down the pile and was turning to go. 'Yes?'

'I know this is a bad time to say it, but I'm going to have to leave here.' She took a deep breath. 'Of course I'll look after Carslake while you're away, but during your absence I'll be making moves to find another position.'

Hugh was suddenly still. 'Why?'

'You know why,' Leah said softly. She moved out from behind her desk. 'Because I love you and I can't live with your bitterness.'

He met her eyes, his reflecting anger. 'Love!' he said scornfully. 'What's love?' He put his hands out and gripped her shoulders. 'I still want you, Leah. Isn't that enough?'

She shook her head in misery. 'No, Hugh.'

He laughed cynically. 'Love? You think it's something separate from physical attraction, something on a higher plane. I've got news for you, Leah Craig. It doesn't exist.'

'It does,' she said stubbornly.

'Like hell it does.' His grip on her shoulders tightened. 'Where's your family, then?' he mocked. 'In all the time you've been here you've never mentioned them. You don't need them any more, isn't that right? Love!' He spat the word out. 'Fine if it's convenient and fits in with what Leah Craig wants to do now.'

Leah gasped. She drew back in shock, staring in stunned amazement at this accusing figure in front of her. His cynical face laughed, mocking her. Before she could help herself her hand drew back and slapped him hard across the cheek. The echo of the slap sounded harshly around the little room.

'Get out of here!' she spat. 'Get out of this room. You say your family is heartless but you're just as bad as they are. Get out.'

He held his hand up to where the mark of her hand could still be seen.

'Perhaps I'm learning,' he agreed harshly. He turned to leave.

'Hugh.' Leah said it quietly.

Hugh stopped at the door but didn't turn back to her.

'I won't be here when you return,' Leah continued quietly. 'I'll stay while you're away but for no longer.'

'As you wish.'

Then he was gone and Leah was free to bury her head in the hated paperwork and give way to her despair.

CHAPTER THIRTEEN

THE next few weeks were the hardest Leah had ever experienced. As the only doctor she found that the work was solid and unrelenting, and that the responsibility of being completely on her own was exhausting in itself. There had always been someone to call on in an emergency. At City Central there were the consultants. At Carslake, until now, there had been Hugh.

For the first time there was no one to ask, no one waiting in the wings to bail her out when she got into difficulties. As Leah worked, the knowledge of her isolation hung over her head like a worrisome cloud.

Added to her burden was the pain of Hugh's departure. She didn't intend being at Carslake when he returned, and the anger of their last meeting would stay with her forever. The memory of his cruel words was locked in her heart, refusing to loosen its grip of misery.

On the Sunday after Hugh's departure Leah had the first couple of hours' freedom since he had left. Her ward round took all morning as all the patients in the hospital were hers, but there was nothing waiting for her as she saw the last patient. With relief she made her way back to the farm. She was mentally and physically exhausted.

'Please let there not be a call back,' she asked aloud as she turned in the farm gate. Her surgery for Monday was fully booked already and the week looked like being relentless.

She made herself a sandwich and then went outside to talk to Dora. The sheep approached her. She stopped before she reached Leah and regarded her balefully.

'I know,' Leah said wearily. 'I've been ignoring you. How your ex-master ever had the time to do what I'm doing plus run a farm is beyond me.' She looked up and met the sheep's accusing stare. 'All right, all right. I'm sorry. He may be super-powered, but I'm not.'

She put out an appeasing hand and Dora approached to nuzzle her affably. Apparently all was forgiven. Beside her, Henry wiggled his backside in agreement.

Leah finished her sandwich and lay back on the grass. The sound of the wind and the calling of the birds in the trees was all she wanted. She was bone weary, she acknowledged, weary with something other than pure physical tiredness.

She hadn't heard from Hugh. For a moment she let herself wonder how his father was and then blocked the thought. Anything to do with Hugh Kendall was none of her business.

The sound of a car on the road above the farm made her raise her head and, with dismay, she realised the car was slowing at her gate. She pushed herself to her feet as a battered sedan made its placid way down the track. Before it came to a stop Leah had recognised the occupant. Mrs Ross.

'Are you coming over to the Harveys'?' Mrs Ross had wound down the window and stopped where Leah stood.

Leah grimaced. She had forgotten all about her promise to visit Wilf and Edith. She shook her head. 'Would you mind giving my excuses?' she asked wearily. 'To be honest, Mrs Ross, I'm really tired.'

That lady gave her a direct stare. 'Are you going to bed?' she demanded.

'N. . .no,' Leah admitted. 'I was going to sit under a tree and read a book.'

'Sit under a tree and brood, more like!' Mrs Ross snorted. 'Come on. Wilf and Edith are expecting you and I told my Walter he couldn't come because I was taking you.' She gestured to the back seat. 'Since he ripped the back seat out so he could take his chooks to the local show I can't take any more than one passenger. And you're it.'

Leah smiled but shook her head. 'I'm on call,' she protested.

'And Dr Kendall didn't leave the radio?'

Leah flung up her hands in capitulation. 'Mrs Ross, I give in. Let's go.'

She was glad she did. The sight of Wilf gave her real pleasure.

She wouldn't have recognised him. The swollen, misshapen face had gone, leaving a face that was weather-beaten, craggy and normal.

'Is it like it was?' she asked Edith delightedly.

Edith laughed. 'I think they've done a wonderful job,' she admitted. 'In fact it's almost too good. He used to have a kink in his nose and they've straightened it. I guess he's more handsome this way, but I sort of liked the kink.'

'Women!' Wilf groaned. 'They're never satisfied.'

Edith linked her arm in his and beamed at Leah. 'It's lovely to have you here,' she told Leah. 'I've spent the morning baking and we've got a proper Sunday afternoon tea, but first Wilf's got a job for you to do.'

'For me?' Leah asked, bemused.

Wilf smiled, his facial muscles still moving stiffly in his healing body. 'I've hooked the plough up to the tractor,' he admitted. 'The dratted City doctors say I'm not allowed on it for at least another six weeks. All I want is about six furrows ploughed in the home paddock so I can put in some spuds, and Mother says you've put in a request to ride on the tractor. I thought I'd kill two birds with the one stone.'

'But I wanted a ride, not to drive the thing,' Leah said in alarm. 'Look where driving it got you.'

Wilf grinned sheepishly. 'It was just being greedy that got me into trouble,' he admitted. 'I was trying to plough land that wasn't meant to be ploughed. It was just too darn steep. The home paddock is as flat as a pancake and the controls are dead easy. Come and see.'

Leah's protests were overruled. They left Edith and Mrs Ross watching from the Harvey's front veranda, and made their way into the home paddock.

Wilf was right. It was easy. Wilf showed her the controls, leaned back on his crutches and cheered her on.

After the first few moments' anxiety Leah found herself relaxing. The noise and power of the big engine blocked out everything else. It was slow, methodical and soothing work. Behind her the ground turned from flattened grass to chocolate-brown furrows.

The first row of furrows was a wobbly mishmash. Leah grimaced as she turned back the way she had come and saw how crooked she had gone. She settled back to make the next one better. By the time she had done six she was almost straight.

Wilf came over as she slowed the big machine.

'Don't stop now,' he ordered. He motioned at the

big clods of broken earth. 'I can't plant spuds in there. Go over it about a couple of times, until it's good and smooth.'

Leah nodded and took her foot off the brake. She was enjoying herself. Suddenly from the big gum-trees surrounding the house came a cloud of white cockatoos, wheeling and screeching above her head. They settled in a mass on the newly ploughed earth and got down to the serious business of searching for grubs and insect life disturbed by Leah's ploughing. As the tractor lumbered towards them they rose with reluctance, settling back on the same earth as soon as she had passed.

From the veranda of the house Edith and Mrs Ross watched with pleasure. Leah glanced across at them and wondered briefly if Mrs Ross had talked to the Harveys about her problems. She shelved the thought. For whatever reason they were doing this, it was a therapy she desperately needed. She waved and got back to the serious business of keeping her furrows straight.

Afterwards there was the promised afternoon tea. Edith had celebrated her return to the farm with a feast of cooking. The table was groaning with tiny sandwiches, a feather-light ginger fluff, a chocolate sponge, lamingtons and scones with jam and cream. Leah had eaten on the run for the last week and had not been hungry. After the fresh air and among these people she found the appetite which she thought had disappeared with Hugh.

'We'll have you entering the ploughing competitions soon,' Wilf chuckled. He too was making up for lost time and was busy with his third piece of chocolate sponge.

'Ploughing competitions?'

Wilf nodded. 'A combination of fastest and straightest.' He grinned self-consciously. 'I got the trophy six years running,' he confessed.

'Well you won't get it this year,' his wife retorted. 'It'll be all over the district that you can't keep the tractor upright.' She smiled at Leah. 'Perhaps you could take over as the next champion. You've time before August to do a bit of practising.'

Leah returned her smile but shook her head. She put down the plate she was holding. Suddenly her appetite had disappeared again.

'I won't be here in August,' she said quietly. 'I'm leaving as soon as Dr Kendall returns.'

There was a momentary silence in the room. Mrs Ross had been talking about her, Leah thought. They accepted her words with no surprise, only sadness. After a moment Edith asked about Mrs Ross's latest grandchild and the conversation moved to more comfortable topics.

The radio came to life as they were about to go. Leah sighed. Her time of peace was at an end. She rang the hospital. A drip had come out and needed to be re-inserted.

'I'll drop you off at your place and you can go in your own car,' Mrs Ross offered. 'I'd better be getting back to Walter. He'll be looking for his tea.'

'It's one thing I won't be looking for,' Leah smiled. She turned to Wilf and Edith. 'Thank you,' she said simply. 'I needed this afternoon.'

'You're more than welcome, child,' Edith said warmly. Her face clouded. 'I just wish there was more we could do.' She reached behind her to a shelf and took down a large, tissue-wrapped parcel. 'This is for you,' she said. 'Think of us when you wear it.'

Leah opened it. Out came a soft blue and white jacket, superbly knitted with an intricate design of intertwined leaves running through it. Leah recognised it as the work Edith had been doing at City Central. She buried her face in its softness with pleasure. She looked up at the elderly couple in front of her and no words came. Her eyes filled with tears.

'Ready?' Mrs Ross asked.

Leah nodded mutely. She stepped forward and planted a kiss firmly on Edith's cheek and then did the same to Wilf. Then she climbed in to Mrs Ross's car, still hugging the jacket. Her three hours off was over. Her weekend was finished.

It was three weeks before Leah heard from Hugh. She was mid-clinic, with a patient undressed on the examining couch, when the phone rang. She apologised to Mr Burt, an elderly farmer with back pain, and picked up the phone. Rosie didn't put calls through when she was with a patient unless they were urgent. It was Hugh.

'Dad died last night. I'll be back on Saturday.' His voice was faint and far away.

'I'm sorry, Hugh,' she said quietly.

'Leah——'

'Is there anything else?' she cut him off. 'I'm with a patient.'

There was a drawn-out pause. 'No,' he said finally. 'I'll see you on Saturday.'

'I won't be here.' She took a deep breath. 'Goodbye, Hugh.' She put down the receiver and turned back to Mr Burt.

* * *

On Friday Leah finished up at the hospital. For part of Saturday, until Hugh returned, there wouldn't be a doctor at Carslake. She couldn't help that. There was no way she would risk meeting him again. It was late at night before she saw her last patient but she stayed and cleared her desk, then wrote meticulous notes on each patient in the hospital. It was fortunate that she had no desperately ill patients in at the moment. There was no one who should need attention until the next evening.

'I'll be at the farm until early tomorrow morning,' she told Matron. She handed her a slip of paper with the name of a city hotel on it. 'After that if there's anything you need me for urgently you can ring me there. As soon as I've found somewhere more permanent I'll let you know.' The hospital would need to be able to contact her in case there was any query about patients she had treated.

She had said her goodbyes to Mrs Ross over hospital dinner. Both of them had found it difficult. Now she turned and walked out of the hospital doors for the last time. Her work at Carslake was over.

The next morning she closed the farm with a heavy heart. She wanted to leave early as there was no way she wanted to risk meeting Hugh. Her luggage was in the back of the ute. She was ready to go.

There was one last job remaining to be done. She walked to the passenger side of the ute and called Dora. As Dora approached suspiciously Leah took hold of her by two handfuls of wool and heaved her into the front seat. Henry went in after her.

It was a cramped trip over to Hugh's farm. Dora had been born in the wrong form as a sheep, Leah decided. She should have been a person or, at the very least, a dog. She settled down to enjoy her short ride. Her fat body took up three quarters of the available room, and Henry wiggled around a sizeable part of the rest, but she was determined to investigate every nook and cranny of the cramped cabin.

'You know, if you kept still and looked at the road we might just survive this trip,' Leah muttered grimly as Dora attempted her fourth complete turn. Henry appeared under his mother's legs and launched himself on to Leah's lap. 'Oh, good grief.' She put her foot on the brake and hauled Henry back from the open window.

'I can't shut the window,' she explained as Henry protested. 'I hate to be personal, but you two smell. Dora, why do I have to have your backside in my face?'

She reached Hugh's road gate with a sigh of relief. As she got out to open the gate Dora looked around suspiciously.

'That's right,' Leah said firmly. 'You've come home. I'm afraid it's back to being a sheep for you, Dora. Just as it's back to being a city doctor for me.' She put a hand on the sheep's nose. They were both fated to be where neither of them wanted to be.

Leah pulled up past the house. As the paddock dropped to the river she could see Hugh's flock grazing peacefully in the morning sun. She went around and opened the passenger door.

'Come on, Dora.'

Henry jumped out and started sniffing the new grass. Dora stayed where she was.

'Come on.'

Dora looked out dubiously. Obviously this place wasn't to her taste. She turned away and laboriously manoeuvred herself so that her backside was presented to Leah. Leah sighed, grabbed the sheep and pulled. Dora dug in her feet and squatted. She stayed exactly where she was.

'Look, you stupid sheep, they won't take you in a city hotel,' Leah said savagely. 'Besides, there's no grass. Now, will you get out?' She braced herself and pulled as hard as she could. Dora didn't move.

'Can I help?'

The soft burr sounded right behind her. Leah froze into immobility. It was Hugh.

'Can I help?' He repeated his question, his voice warm with amusement.

Leah didn't look behind her. 'You can get your stupid sheep out of my car,' she said tightly.

'Sure.' He walked around and opened the driver's door, then came back and edged Leah aside. 'Go on, you great lump,' he said firmly to Dora, prodding her hard in her rear. Dora looked behind her, gave him a baleful glance and lumbered forward, over the gearstick and out of the car. 'Anything else, ma'am?' He turned back to Leah.

Leah looked stonily up at him. 'You weren't supposed to come back until today.'

'No,' he agreed equitably. 'If I'd said I was returning on Friday, though, Dr Leah Craig would have left on Thursday. Wouldn't she?'

'Yes.'

'Well, then.' The matter was clearly explained to Hugh's satisfaction.

Leah sighed. She walked around to the driver's door of her ute. 'If you were aiming to see me, then you've seen me,' she said.

Hugh slid into the passenger seat beside her. He

reached over and took the keys from the ignition switch. 'Leah, we need to talk.'

'We've said everything we could possibly say to each other,' she said quietly. She held out her hand. 'I want my keys, please.'

He reached across and placed a hand on her shoulder. The feel of his fingers sent fire through Leah's body and she pulled back.

'Don't touch me.' Anger was her only weapon against this man. She had to use it. If she let her emotion hold sway she would be in his arms, helpless against the tide of longing sweeping over her. She had let her emotions rule her for too long. From here on in she had to listen to her head.

'Leah, listen to me——'

'No.' She threw the word at him as if it were a solid object. 'Get out.' She grabbed the keys back from his hand and glared at him. As she did a new sound broke the stillness. From the house came the strident ring of the telephone.

'There you go, then,' she said cruelly. 'There's no other doctor at Carslake apart from you now. If they're looking for you already it'll be an emergency, as I left the routine work cleared up.'

'Leah. . .' His hand gripped her urgently, his eyes holding her. 'Stay.'

'You'd better answer it,' she said calmly.

Their eyes met for a long moment. The ringing continued. Finally Hugh broke. The conditioning to emergencies was too strong.

Leah watched as he strode up the veranda steps. As he disappeared inside the house she turned on the ignition. She didn't look back.

CHAPTER FOURTEEN

THE road from the valley passed in a blur. Leah drove slowly, forced by her tears to slacken her pace.

Damn him for being there. It had been a month since she had seen him. A month. The pain had dulled from a bitter stab to a raw ache. Now the piercing agony was back, as fierce as it had ever been.

How long would it stay with her? How long before she couldn't see those blue eyes, feel the brush of his chin against her cheek whenever she closed her eyes?

She thought back to the self-contained Leah Craig from City Central, with her life all neatly planned. Perhaps she had been stupid to throw away her ordered existence. Love. Hugh derided it. Perhaps he was right.

She angrily brushed away tears and tried to concentrate on the road. Along here was the Harveys' where it had all started, with Edith standing in the road. . .

She was there again.

This time Edith wasn't risking her life. She was standing at the edge of the road, but there was no missing her. She held a bright red tea-towel and waved it fiercely as Leah's little vehicle approached.

Leah slowed and stopped. She brushed her eyes again. There was no disguising the fact that she had been crying. She climbed out into the road. Remembering the last time this had happened, she asked sharply, 'What is it, Edith? Wilf?'

Edith shook her head. She approached Leah, her sharp eyes taking in Leah's dishevelled appearance.

'Dr Kendall phoned,' she said gently. 'He asked if we could try to stop you.'

'Oh.' Leah stared blankly at the lady in front of her. What possible motive could Hugh have for doing this?

'The hospital has just contacted him.' Edith's voice was still expressionless, her eyes on Leah's face. 'A child's come in with appendicitis. Matron's pretty sure it's already burst.'

Appendicitis! The hospital needed her! For a moment Leah had to suppress a wild urge to laugh. What did she have to do to get away from here?

'I've left,' Leah said harshly.

'Dr Kendall says if he can't operate the child will die. He says according to Matron he's going to be lucky if he can save her anyway.'

'Oh, God.' Leah turned away and buried her face in her hands. It was a nightmare that wouldn't end.

'You'll go?'

'Yes.' Leah's voice dragged. 'I'll go.'

Edith nodded. She put a hand out and touched Leah's cheek. 'Come in and have a wash while I phone and tell them you're on your way. It'll make you feel better.'

With an effort Leah dredged up a smile. 'Thank you.' She gestured to her face. 'I don't know what I look like.'

Edith regarded her with compassion. 'You look as if you might be making the wrong decision,' she said.

By the time Leah walked into the operating theatre the child had been prepped and the anaesthetic administered. Hugh was simply waiting for her to take over the anaesthetics before he could begin.

He barely acknowledged her arrival and one look at the child on the table told Leah why. It was going to take their combined skills and an awful lot of luck to get the little girl through.

They worked steadily, each totally absorbed in the job at hand. For the moment the conflict between them had disappeared as they came together in this common purpose. Their skills blended, each anticipating what the other required. Not for the first time Leah found herself marvelling at the dexterity of Hugh's fingers. They gave hope to the little girl on the table.

At last Hugh could do no more. The last of the mess that had been an appendix was cleared out of the little abdomen. Now all they could hope was that the child could find the strength to fight back.

'How did she get into this state?' Leah asked as Hugh started to close.

'Her parents don't believe in doctors,' Hugh said shortly. 'They tried herbal remedies for three days.'

Leah grimaced.

With a drainage tube inserted and antibiotic already feeding into the little arm they were finished. The child was wheeled into the recovery ward. Leah and Hugh started to peel off their surgical gowns.

'Do you think she'll make it?' Leah asked.

Hugh nodded. 'I think I've managed to get it clean. Clean enough to give her a fighting chance anyway, and, given her age and health, that's probably all that she needs.'

There was silence again as they washed.

'Leah?' Hugh turned to her as she finished drying her hands.

'Yes.' Her voice was expressionless. She felt as though she were wrung out, incapable of more emotion.

'Leah, I have to talk to the parents and I can't leave

the hospital until she's fully conscious.' He took her arm and turned her to face him. 'Leah, I really need to talk to you. Will you go back to my place and wait for me?'

'Why should I?'

'Because I'm asking you to.' His tone was urgent. 'Please, Leah.'

'Or you'll set Edith out on the road again.'

He smiled. 'No. I wouldn't do that.' He hesitated. 'Leah, I've been a bloody fool. Please, allow me at least the time to apologise.'

'There's no need.' Leah's voice was dull.

'There is.' Matron appeared at the door behind them and he lowered his voice urgently. 'I have to go. Will you wait?'

Leah looked at him for a long moment. Finally she nodded.

His expression lightened. 'The back door's open. Make yourself a cup of tea. I'll be there when I can.'

It was strange sitting in Hugh's kitchen, waiting for him to come home. The house was very much his home, furnished simply with big, comfortable furniture and scattered with his belongings.

Leah perused his bookcase. There were travel books, books of poetry, whodunits, a weird assortment of fun and serious reading. Leah fingered the books thoughtfully. This collection must cost him a huge effort to pack and move, she thought, thinking of her sparse belongings in the ute outside. He obviously considered he was here to stay. Leah read only library books. Since she was thirteen she had moved from one place to another. The trouble of moving possessions had started to outweigh the pleasure of owning them.

It was after lunchtime. She searched in the refrigerator and found that Hugh had restocked it. There was
more than enough for her to cook something interesting. Hugh would be a while, she guessed. She was
better off to keep busy.

Why was she staying? As she put together the
ingredients for a quiche she tried to sort out the reasons
in her head. In the end she gave up. She knew only
that it was important to Hugh and, for some reason,
she had given her word that she would.

By the time she heard Hugh approaching the quiche
was ready, steaming and fragrant. A tossed French
salad was on the table, with bread that Leah had found
in the freezer and heated to crusty warmth. Hugh
strode up the veranda steps and stopped at the door,
his nose registering the preparations.

'Lunch,' he said appreciatively. He smiled at Leah
and her heart did its familiar lurch. 'What have you
been doing?'

'Making a quiche,' she said self-consciously. 'You
can just have bread and salad if you like.'

'Why can't I have quiche?'

'Haven't you heard the saying?' Leah smiled. '"Real
men don't eat quiche."'

'Real men can't be very hungry, then,' he retorted,
coming in. 'And they obviously haven't smelt Dr Leah
Craig's quiche.' He opened the refrigerator and produced a bottle of moselle. 'A lunch like this deserves a
wine.' He searched in the cupboard for a corkscrew
and two wine glasses, bringing them to the table where
Leah was serving.

'How is she?' Leah asked.

'Conscious again,' Hugh said briefly. 'I think she'll

make it. I've had to spend some time with the parents. They're blaming themselves.'

'As they ought.'

'Well, sometimes I wonder which is worse,' Hugh replied. 'This couple went to extremes, but then you get the opposite—the child who gets brought in three times in the course of a head cold.'

They lapsed into silence for a while, concentrating on their food. Leah felt her self-consciousness increasing. Once she risked a quick glance up, only to find Hugh's eyes on her, warm with understanding. With burning cheeks she looked away again.

'I am sorry about your father,' she finally managed to say. 'It must have been a bad time.'

Hugh finished the last piece of quiche on his plate. He reached for his wine glass and pushed his chair back from the table.

'It was,' he said finally. He stared reflectively into the glass he was holding. 'There was a lot I had to come to terms with.'

'Such as?'

He sighed. 'When I arrived there was no one to meet me. I went straight to the hospital. They were right. Dad was dying. He was conscious, but only just.' He paused. 'One of the horrible things about being a doctor is that you know what to expect. He knew what was happening.'

'Was he pleased to see you?' Leah asked.

'He was,' Hugh said quietly. He gave a bitter laugh. 'Illness does strange things to people.'

'And your mother?'

'I wouldn't know.' Hugh gave the same laugh. 'She was much too busy to spend any time with me. Or with Dad either, for that matter. When she came back from her conference she had a huge backlog of work to catch up with, as well as having to fit in a couple of compulsory visits to my father a day. She had to do that,' he said bitterly. 'People expected it.' He grimaced. 'And my brothers found it convenient that Dad was in hospital. They could fit him in on their ward rounds.'

Leah was silent for a moment. Finally she found the courage to continue.

'You spent time with him though?'

'I took him home.' Hugh rose and started clearing the plates. 'It was all he wanted to do. All his life he's been an avid gardener. Our home is surrounded by a magnificent garden which is a credit to him. He wanted to spend his last days where he could see it.'

'And he did?'

'He had eight days back in his beloved garden before the stroke that killed him.' He stared reflectively at the blank wall in front of him. 'He had his garden and me. It was all he had. I had to fight to get my mother and brothers to agree to let him come home. It was much more convenient for them to have him in hospital. After he was home my mother saw him late at night when he was usually sleeping, and my brothers dropped in a couple of times during their lunch hours.'

He ran the water into the sink. 'They came to the funeral of course,' he finally continued. 'The lovely Jane was there too. Do you remember me telling you about Jane? My ex-fiancée? She came to pay her respects.'

Leah stirred uneasily. She picked up a tea-towel and started drying the dishes that Hugh was washing. She could think of nothing to say.

'I've learned something, Leah,' Hugh went on conversationally. 'I've been judging the human race by a group of people that's different.'

He put the plate he was washing on to the rack and turned to her. He took the towel from her and dried his hands. 'Come on,' he said roughly. 'Leave these. Let's go down to the river.'

Leah looked at her watch. 'If I'm going to get to the city before dark I'd better leave soon,' she warned.

'I'll have you home before dark,' he said. Leah looked up wonderingly but his face was expressionless. Mentally she shrugged her shoulders. She was past making decisions for herself.

They walked slowly down through the paddocks, Hugh setting the pace and Leah walking at his side. Her mind was racing over unformed questions. She stole a look at the man by her side and then looked away. A shred of hope was blossoming. She tried to suppress it but it would not die. He was different.

As they reached the track leading down through the bush to the river-bank he took her hand, guiding her through.

As the track ended, where the bank fell away sharply to the flowing river below, they stopped. A log had fallen near the track. On its south side a bed of soft green moss had formed. Hugh sank down on it, pulling Leah down to sit beside him.

'You didn't bring the radio receiver,' Leah suddenly remembered.

'No,' he said easily. 'I didn't.'

'That's not like the conscientious Hugh Kendall,' Leah smiled.

'The conscientious Hugh Kendall will be back on

deck tomorrow morning. For this afternoon I've told Matron she's without a doctor.'

'Hugh!'

'Leah!' he mimicked. He paused, then asked seriously, 'Leah, what happened to your parents?'

Leah looked up, meeting his eyes. 'They were killed when I was thirteen.'

He nodded. 'They had to be. I figured it out during the long nights I spent sitting by my father's bed. And your great-uncle? Did he reject you?'

'Yes.' Briefly she told him what had happened. When she finished there was a long silence.

'I knew it,' he said finally. 'How could I have been so blind? All the time I was in Scotland I kept looking at my family and the people they were associated with and thinking, this is not Leah. These people are different. They're callous, hard and greedy. Because they were my family I've never been able to see them clearly as people apart. It was only coming straight from you to go to them that made me realise.'

'Realise what?' Her voice was a whisper.

He turned and took her hands into his. For a moment he studied them, stroking the smooth skin. 'That you could never be like that,' he said simply, looking up. 'My lovely Leah who trusted me with her body and her heart, only to have that trust repaid with cynicism and distrust. I should have known. . . The first time I met you I should have known. My cynical head was telling me one thing and every other part of me was screaming another.'

He let go of one of her hands and placed his to lie his palm against her cheek.

'Leah, you've told me before that you love me. Have I killed that love?'

A tiny throb of happiness was starting at the back of Leah's head. It was like a muted drum, echoing the rhythm of her heart. Tears were starting in her eyes. Mutely she shook her head.

He took her face between both hands and searched her tear-filled eyes. 'Leah, I love you,' he said gently. 'I would trust you with my life. I've been a fool but I'm asking you to give me another chance.' He stopped, and kissed the tears from her cheeks. 'Leah, my heart, will you marry me?'

Leah couldn't speak. The tears flowed unchecked down her face. Her whole being was dissolving in a mist of happiness and love.

'Leah!' He held her face and pulled it up so that her eyes were meeting his. His voice was urgent with desire. 'Will you marry me?'

Leah put her fingers up and touched the beloved face. She pulled him down so that their lips met, lightly at first and then in a hungry sealing of their longing. For minutes they stayed, neither wanting to break the moment.

Finally they drew apart. Leah's tears had stopped, but her eyes still glistened with their moisture. Her voice trembled as she found the words to speak.

'Yes, my love,' she said with certainty. 'I'll marry you.'

Mills & Boon

Discover the thrill of 4 Exciting Medical Romances – FREE

FREE

BOOKS FOR YOU

In the exciting world of modern medicine, the emotions of true love have an added drama. Now you can experience four of these unforgettable romantic tales of passion and heartbreak FREE – and look forward to a regular supply of Mills & Boon Medical Romances delivered direct to your door!

🐦 🐦 🐦

Turn the page for details of 2 extra free gifts, and how to apply.

An Irresistible Offer from Mills & Boon

Here's an offer from Mills & Boon to become a regular reader of Medical Romances. To welcome you, we'd like you to have four books, a cuddly teddy and a special MYSTERY GIFT, all absolutely free and without obligation.

Then, every month you could look forward to receiving 4 more **brand new** Medical Romances for £1.45 each, delivered direct to your door, post and packing free. Plus our newsletter featuring author news, competitions, special offers, and lots more.

This invitation comes with no strings attached. You can cancel or suspend your subscription at any time, and still keep your free books and gifts.

Its so easy. Send no money now. Simply fill in the coupon below and post it at once to -

**Mills & Boon Reader Service, FREEPOST,
PO Box 236, Croydon, Surrey CR9 9EL**

NO STAMP REQUIRED

- ✂ -

YES! Please rush me my 4 Free Medical Romances and 2 Free Gifts! Please also reserve me a Reader Service Subscription. If I decide to subscribe, I can look forward to receiving 4 brand new Medical Romances every month for just £5.80, delivered direct to my door. Post and packing is free, and there's a free Mills & Boon Newsletter. If I choose not to subscribe I shall write to you within 10 days - I can keep the books and gifts whatever I decide. I can cancel or suspend my subscription at any time. I am over 18.

EP03D

Name (Mr/Mrs/Ms) _____

Address _____

_____

_____ Postcode _____

Signature_____